TRAVIS DAVENTHORPE
POWERS UP!

BY
WES MOLEBASH

:01
First Second
NEW YORK

Published by First Second
First Second is an imprint of Roaring Brook Press,
a division of Holtzbrinck Publishing Holdings Limited Partnership
120 Broadway, New York, NY 10271
firstsecondbooks.com
mackids.com

Library of Congress Control Number: 2023937710

First edition, 2024
Edited by Robyn Chapman and Michael Moccio
Cover and interior book design by Casper Manning
Series design by Molly Johanson
Production editing by Kat Kopit and Nora Milman
Special thanks to David Bowles and Kira Aitch

Drawn and colored in Procreate with a pencil-style digital nib and inked with a brush-style digital nib. Dialogue, word balloons, and other finishing touches were added in Photoshop. The lettering is a mix of hand lettering and a custom font composed of the artist's handwriting.

Printed in China by 1010 Printing International Limited, Kwun Tong, Hong Kong

ISBN 978-1-250-80143-2 (paperback)
10 9 8 7 6 5 4 3 2 1

ISBN 978-1-250-80142-5 (hardcover)
10 9 8 7 6 5 4 3 2 1

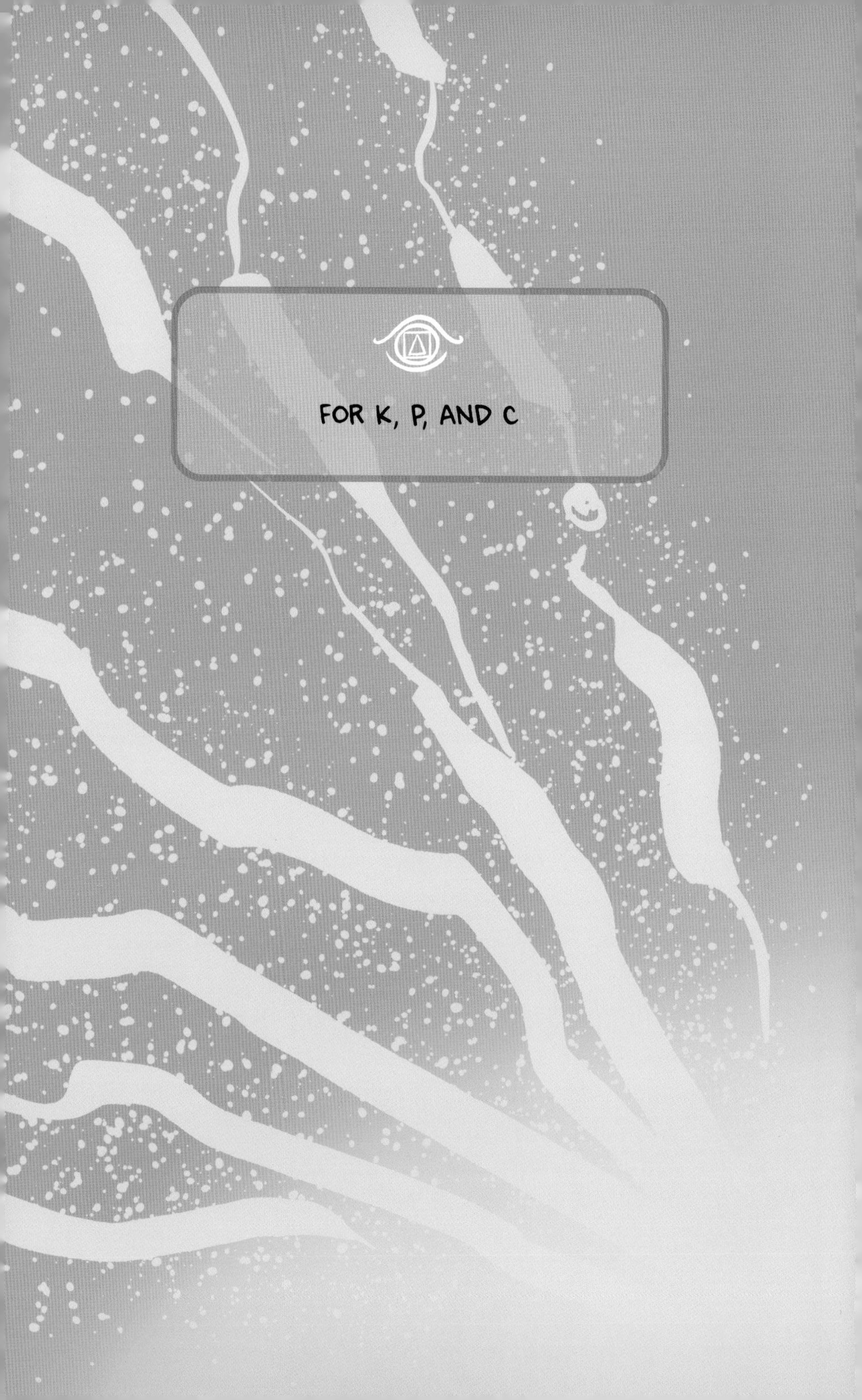

FOR K, P, AND C

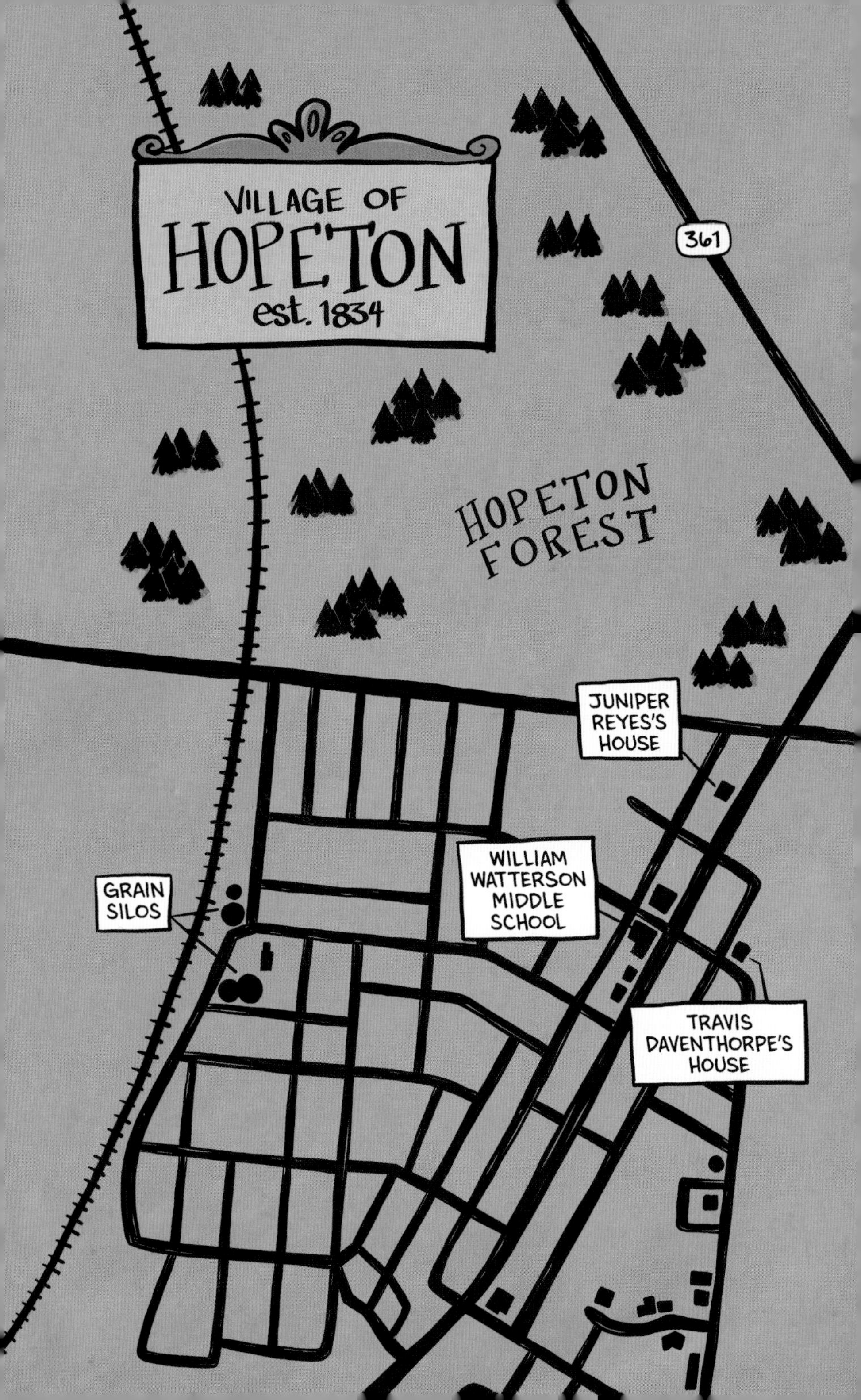
VILLAGE OF
HOPETON
est. 1834
361
HOPETON
FOREST
JUNIPER
REYES'S
HOUSE
WILLIAM
WATTERSON
MIDDLE
SCHOOL
GRAIN
SILOS
TRAVIS
DAVENTHORPE'S
HOUSE

159
THOMAS HOPE
FOUNDER
COUNTY LINE ROAD
N
NW
NE
W
E
SW
SE
S
CARL'S
FARM

WHAT HAPPENED TO THE BLACK HOLE, CARL?! IT WAS RIGHT HERE A FEW DAYS AGO!

NOW DON'T YOU WORRY, BOBBY!
FEED
OIL

JUST WATCH WALTER AND ME!
OIL

BLUE FIFTY-TWO!
OIL

BLUE FIFTY-TWO!
OIL

HUT! HUT!

OIL

WHAT? ARE YOU JUST TRYING TO SHOW ME YOU CAN STILL THROW A TIGHT SPIRAL?

VOOOSH

IT'S STILL THERE!

NOW LISTEN TO ME, BOBBY! I AIN'T PART OF THE CPA...
CIA.

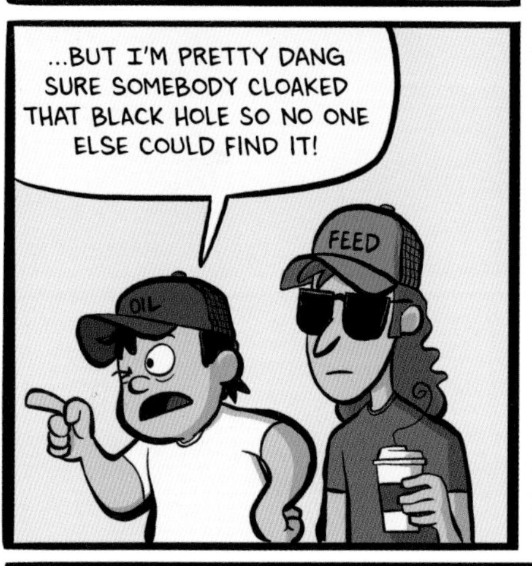
...BUT I'M PRETTY DANG SURE SOMEBODY CLOAKED THAT BLACK HOLE SO NO ONE ELSE COULD FIND IT!

WHATEVER, CARL.

BIG SNOW'S S'POSED TO BE COMIN' IN THIS WEEK.
WE'RE DUE. WE'RE DUE.

OKAY, JUNIPER...
WHY ARE WE PLAYING
THIS GAME?
BECAUSE, TRAVIS, THERE'S NOTHING ELSE TO DO AFTER LUNCH BESIDES SIT ON THE BLEACHERS AND DO HOMEWORK.
THAT SOUNDS LIKE FUN TO ME.

ALSO BECAUSE BELA WANTS YOU TO PARTICIPATE IN MORE PHYSICAL ACTIVITY. HE SAYS IT'LL HELP WITH YOUR SWORD TRAINING.

FINE. WHATEVER.
WELL, IF IT ISN'T THE **LOSER** OF THE WILLIAM WATTERSON MIDDLE SCHOOL SCIENCE FAIR!

NOT THIS AGAIN.
HERE COMES DEREK.

HOW HARD WAS IT GETTING OUT OF BED THIS MORNING...

...KNOWING THE BEAKMAN PRIZE IS SITTING ON **MY** SHELF?

WHATEVER! WE BOTH KNOW YOU CHEATED TO WIN THAT PRIZE!

REALLY? DO WE **BOTH** KNOW THAT?

LATER, **DAVENTWERP.** SEE YOU ON THE COURT.

I CAN'T STAND THAT GUY!
HE'S JUST TRYING TO GET UNDER YOUR SKIN, TRAVIS.
HERE. TAKE A BALL.
SO WHAT THE HECK IS THIS GAME CALLED AGAIN?
SPEEDBALL. IT COMBINES FOOTBALL, SOCCER, AND BASKETBALL.
I DON'T KNOW WHY I ASKED. IT'S LIKE YOU'RE SPEAKING A FOREIGN LANGUAGE.
LIKE ELVISH?
NO, I UNDERSTAND ELVISH.

FWEET!

ALL RIGHT, LISTEN UP! WE'RE SPLITTING INTO TEAMS!

SCHULZ! TEAM ONE! YOU'RE A FORWARD!
SWEET!

JOHNSTON! TEAM TWO! YOU'RE A FULLBACK!
YAY!

PEARSON! TEAM ONE! YOU'RE A HALFBACK!
OKAY.

DEVERS! TEAM TWO! YOU'RE A FORWARD!
EXCELLENT!

SCHOOL BULLY

DEREK DEVERS

LEVEL 2

HIGH CHARISMA ALLOWS HIM TO LIE AND GET AWAY WITH IT MOST OF THE TIME

BEST ATHLETE IN SCHOOL, AND HE KNOWS IT

FUN FACT:
MOM LABELS HIS UNDERWEAR

SKILLS

STRENGTH	+12
KINDNESS	+0
SPEEDBALL	+8
ACADEMICS	+6
INTIMIDATION	+10

ABILITIES

ATOMIC WEDGIES ★★★
HUMILIATING INSULTS ★★☆
TEACHERS' PET ★☆☆

MATTHEWS! TEAM ONE! FORWARD!
NEELY! TEAM TWO! FULLBACK!
LEWIS! TEAM ONE! FULLBACK!
REYNOLDS! TEAM TWO! HALFBACK!
REYES! TEAM ONE! FORWARD!
YES!

ENGINEERING WHIZ

JUNIPER REYES

LEVEL 2

SUPER SMARTS GIVE TRAVIS A RUN FOR HIS MONEY

LOYAL FRIEND TO THE VERY END

FUN FACT:
SHE WAS BORN IN ARIZONA AFTER HER PARENTS EMIGRATED FROM MEXICO.

SKILLS

INTELLIGENCE	+12
ENGINEERING	+10
SPORTS	+5
GAMING	+7
POPULARITY	+3

ABILITIES

BMX BIKE RIDING	★★★
LEGEND of GRIFF	★★☆
HIGH FIVES	★★★

HAACK! TEAM TWO! FULLBACK!
JONES! TEAM ONE! HALFBACK!
LEE! TEAM TWO! GOALIE!
DAVENTHORPE!

TEAM ONE!

ALSO GOALIE!
WHAT?!

RELUCTANT HERO

TRAVIS DAVENTHORPE

LEVEL 2

SMARTEST KID IN THE WHOLE SCHOOL, BUT HE'S NOT ALL BRAGGY ABOUT IT. WELL, MAYBE A **LITTLE** BRAGGY

STRANGE BIRTHMARK IS THE BUTT OF MANY JOKES, BUT TRAVIS HAS RECENTLY LEARNED TO LOVE IT

FUN FACT:
TRAVIS IS THE PROPHESIED HERO OF SOLUSTERRA, A KINGDOM IN ANOTHER UNIVERSE

SKILLS

INTELLIGENCE	+15
ROBOTICS	+12
COMPUTERS	+10
SPORTS	+0
POPULARITY	−2

ABILITIES

SWORD FIGHTING 
LEGEND of GRIFF ★★★
ROBOT BUILDING ★★★

NOW LET'S PLAY SOME SPEEDBALL!
FWEET!
GO TIGERS

TRAVIS, WHAT ARE YOU DOING?! YOU'RE SUPPOSED TO KEEP THE BALL FROM GOING IN THE NET!
YEAH! LIKE THIS!
DEREK EXECUTES A CRITICAL HIT!

KA POW
OOOF!

THERE YOU GO, **DAVENTWERP!** THAT'S HOW YOU STOP THE BALL!

NO MANCHES. WHAT THE HECK, DUDE?!
POP

WHATEVER. OUR TEAM WON.

WHAT WAS **THAT** ALL ABOUT?

GO TIGERS
DON'T WORRY ABOUT IT. LET'S JUST GET YOU CLOTHED.
THIS WAS A BAD DAY TO WEAR MY ROCKET SHIP UNDERWEAR.

WILLIAM WATTERSON MIDDLE SCHOOL
IT'S SO NICE OUT! I CAN'T BELIEVE IT'S SUPPOSED TO SNOW THIS WEEK!
I KNOW, RIGHT?! THAT'S OHIO WEATHER FOR YA.
SCHOOL BUS
SCHOOL BUS
THE FORECAST SAYS IT'S GONNA DUMP A TON OF SNOW ON US, THOUGH.
MAYBE WE CAN GO SLEDDING! I'VE NEVER DONE THAT BEFORE!
TOTALLY!

SO YOU'RE FOR SURE NOT GOING TO HAVE TRAVBOT FIGHT WITH THE **LEGENDARY SWORD OF LEGENDS?**
IT WASN'T A BAD IDEA, YOU KNOW? IT JUST NEEDS SOME TWEAKS.

NO. I'VE GOT NEW PLANS FOR TRAVBOT.
BESIDES, BELA WANTS **ME** TO USE THE SWORD, SO I'VE BEEN WORKING ON MAKING THAT HAPPEN.

I'M SURE YOU'LL FIGURE IT OUT, TRAV.
THANKS! I THINK I'M CLOSE!
HOPETON VALLEY FOREST ENTRANCE
PICNIC AREA AHEAD

EITHER WAY, TRAVBOT SHOULD BE READY TO TRAIN WITH US IN TIME FOR OUR NEXT PRACTICE! I CAN'T WAIT TO SHOW YOU WHAT HE CAN DO!
ME NEITHER!
RESTROOMS
Magic Flash!

WHERE DO YOU TAKE THEM, BELAZAR?

ABANDONED WAREHOUSE
POUGHKEEPSIE, NEW YORK
TRAVIS! JUNIPER! IT'S WONDERFUL TO SEE YOU!
IT'S GOOD TO SEE YOU, TOO, BELA!

HOW MUCH LIFE IS LEFT IN YOUR GEN 1 ARMOR?
DON'T BE HATING ON MY GEN 1. SHE'S A TOUGH OLD GIRL!

TOUGH? MORE LIKE A **BAG OF BOLTS.**

I SEEM TO REMEMBER THIS **BAG OF BOLTS** KNOCKING YOU AND YOUR SWORD THROUGH THAT **WALL** OVER THERE.

...I DON'T REMEMBER THAT.

THAT'S BECAUSE YOU BLACKED OUT.
IT'S TRUE. I WAS THERE.

AND I REMEMBER THE TUSSLE MAKING QUITE A COMMOTION.

WHICH IS WHY I'VE PLACED A CHARM ON THE WAREHOUSE WHILE WE'RE USING IT.

NO ONE WILL BE ABLE TO HEAR US OR SEE US WHILE WE'RE HERE. NO MATTER HOW VIOLENT IT MAY GET.

SO FEEL FREE TO KNOCK THE BOY THROUGH AS MANY WALLS AS YOU WISH, MS. REYES.

BRIGHT MAGE

BELAZAR

LEVEL 30

AS A BRIGHT MAGE, HE HAS POWERFUL MAGICAL ABILITIES GIFTED HIM BY THE CREATRIX

TRAINED IN A MEDITATIVE MARTIAL ART AS A SPIRITUAL PRACTICE AND SELF-DEFENSE

FUN FACT:
SELECTED
NOL INVICTUS KING
OF SOLUSTERRA
(HUGE MISTAKE)

SKILLS

INTELLIGENCE	+15
STRENGTH	+13
CHARISMA	+15
WISDOM	+15
MAGIC	+15

ABILITIES

CLOAKING	★★★
PERCEIVE EVIL	★★★
DIVINE COURAGE	★★★

HARDY HAR.
WE'LL SEE WHO'S LAUGHING ONCE YOU'VE GOTTEN A LOAD OF MY...
NEURAL STIMULATORS!

SHOULDN'T NEURAL STIMULATORS GO ON YOUR HEAD?

THESE ARE DIFFERENT.

USING PARTS FROM A GAMEBOX CONTROLLER...

...I ADDED BUTTONS THAT WILL ALLOW ME TO FIGHT JUST LIKE GRIFF FROM **LEGEND OF GRIFF!**

I'LL BE THE JUDGE OF THAT.

JUNIPER! ATTACK!

FOR MY FIRST FEAT, ALLOW ME TO SHOW YOU MY...
SHINNG
JUMP SLASH!

WHOOP!
KLANG! KA-KLANG!

STILL FIGURING OUT HOW TO STICK THE LANDING...
heh heh

FOR MY SECOND FEAT, BRACE YOURSELF FOR MY...

SPIN MOVE!
WHOOSH

UGH!

SHOULDN'T HAVE EATEN THOSE LAST COUPLE TATER TOTS AT LUNCH.

FOR MY
FINAL FEAT...

...PREPARE YOURSELVES TO FACE
THE WRATH OF MY...

HACK
ATTACK!
CHOP
CHOP
CHOP
CHOP
CHOP
CHOP
CHOP

STOP! STOP!
FOR THE LOVE OF THE CREATRIX, STOP!
RRAAAAGH
CHUNK CHUNK CHUNK

WOW! THAT WAS QUITE A WORKOUT!
I'LL SAY!
UNFORTUNATELY, I'M NOT SURE WE'RE ANY FURTHER THAN WHEN WE FIRST STARTED.

WHAT ARE YOU TALKING ABOUT? A COUPLE MORE TWEAKS TO THE STIMULATORS, AND WE'RE OFF TO THE RACES!

THERE'S NO QUESTION THAT THE MOVES YOU DISPLAYED ARE QUITE POWERFUL...

...BUT YOU'RE STILL PUTTING TOO MUCH TRUST IN YOUR TECHNOLOGY, TRAVIS.

YOU MUST HAVE FAITH IN THE CREATRIX! TRUST IN THE POWER HE'S GIVEN TO YOU AND THE SWORD!

BUT I'LL NEVER HAVE FAITH LIKE YOU, BELA!
FOR YOU, **FAITH** IS LIFE!
BUT FOR ME, **SCIENCE** IS LIFE!

YOU DON'T HAVE TO CHOOSE BETWEEN SCIENCE AND FAI—

RIGHT! WE HAVE TO COMPROMISE!

AND **THIS** IS THE COMPROMISE.

I'M TRUSTING THE CREATRIX BY USING THE SWORD MYSELF...

...AND THE NEURAL STIMULATORS I DEVELOPED CAN ENHANCE MY SKILL.

BUT YOU HAVE NO **SKILL** TO ENHANCE. THAT'S THE PROB—

BELA.

YOU'RE RIGHT, JUNIPER. I'VE MADE MY POINT.

HEY, IF I SCREW UP TOO BADLY, YOU'LL BE RIGHT THERE TO HELP ME OUT OF A JAM. THAT'S WHY THE CREATRIX SENT YOU.

I MAY NOT ALWAYS BE HERE, TRAVIS.

MY JOB ISN'T TO GUIDE AND PROTECT YOU FOR THE REST OF YOUR LIFE...
...IT'S TO HELP AWAKEN YOU TO THE POWER THE CREATRIX HAS PLACED WITHIN YOU AND THE SWORD.

TRAVIS! WELCOME HOME, SON! HOW WAS FENCING PRACTICE?
YES! TELL US ALL ABOUT IT!

GREAT! I LEARNED SOME NEW MOVES TODAY!

I LEARNED A JUMP SLASH...

...A SPIN MOVE...

...AND A HACK ATTACK!

I ALWAYS THOUGHT FENCING REQUIRED MORE ATHLETICISM AND STRATEGY...

...BUT THAT'S GREAT! YOU'RE LEARNING NEW THINGS!

MOM & DAD

LEVEL 24

MARRIED FOR FOURTEEN YEARS

HAVE MASTERED THE ART OF WORRYING ABOUT EVERYTHING

FUN FACT: MET AT A JAM BAND CONCERT WHEN THEY WERE IN COLLEGE

SKILLS

KINDNESS	+12
PATIENCE	+10
CHARISMA	+ 8
WISDOM	+ 9
NAIVETE	+15

ABILITIES

DAD JOKES

MOM ANXIETY

STYLISHNESS

WELL, I'M GONNA GO UPSTAIRS AND CHECK ON TRAVBOT.
OKAY, HON.

DO YOU THINK TRAVIS IS LYING ABOUT BEING ON THE SCHOOL'S FENCING TEAM?

HA HA HA HA HA
WHO AM I KIDDING? I DON'T KNOW HOW TO DETECT HUMAN EMOTION, LET ALONE LIES!

ANYWAY, I'M PREPARING FOR MY PRE-WINTER-STORM GROCERY TRIP.

PLEASE LET ME KNOW IF YOU'D LIKE ANYTHING ADDED TO THE LIST.

WILL DO, BUTLERBOT.

YES. THANK YOU, BUTLERBOT.

TRAVIS.
LYING.
PFFT.
RIGHT?
heh heh
SILLY TALK.

WHAT'S UP, TRAVBOT! HOW'S THE UPDATE COMING ALONG?
IT'S ALMOST FINISHED, TRAVIS! HOW WAS SWORD TRAINING?

ROBOT

TRAVBOT 2.0

LEVEL 2

FUN FACT:
ONLY KNOWN ROBOT TO HAVE BEEN SWALLOWED BY A CYBORG TYRANNOSAURUS REX

SKILLS

INTELLIGENCE	+16
STRENGTH	+14
KINDNESS	+12
ARMOR	+10
HONESTY	+7

ABILITIES

FLIGHT ★★☆
FRIENDSHIP ★★★
EUCHRE ★★☆

PRETTY GOOD. JUNIPER IS GETTING MORE AND MORE COMFORTABLE WITH HER MECH SUIT. SHE'S DEFINITELY OUR TANK.

BELA IS OUR SPELLCASTER, FOR OBVIOUS REASONS.

AND ONCE YOUR ARM CANNONS ARE CALIBRATED, YOU'LL BE OUR RANGED FIGHTER!

SPEAKING OF WHICH, LET'S TAKE A LOOK.

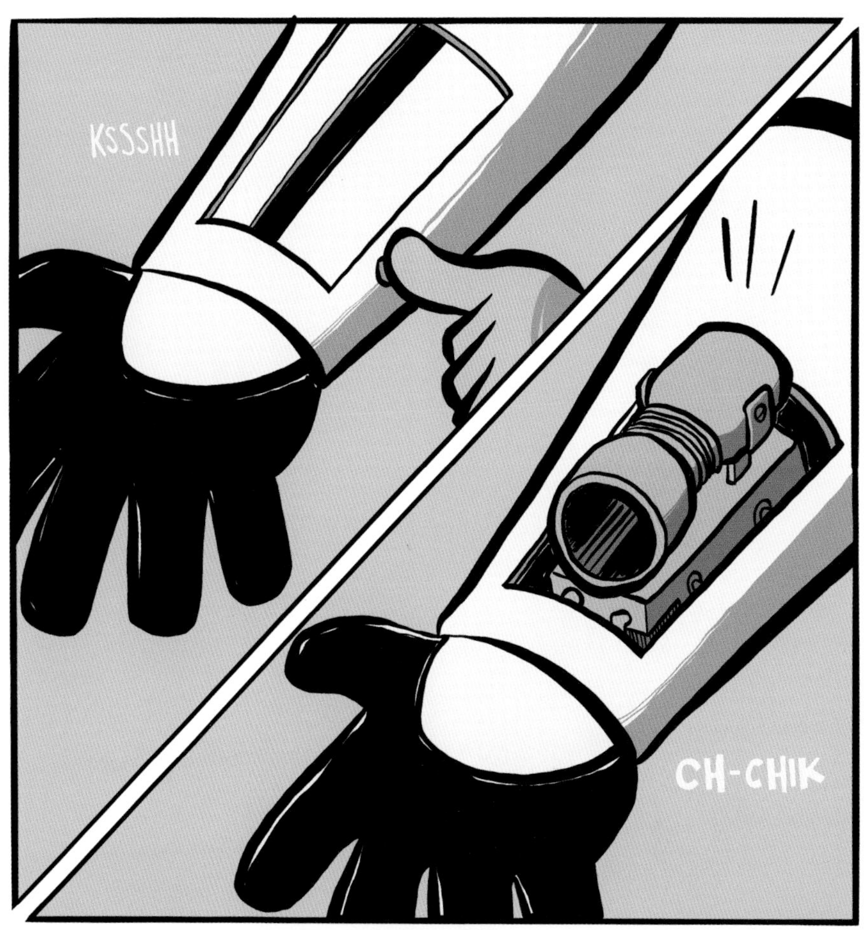
KSSSHH
CH-CHIK

IT NEVER STOPS BEING AWESOME.
IT REALLY DOESN'T.

WHAT ABOUT YOU? WHAT IS YOUR ROLE IN OUR GROUP?

I DON'T KNOW YET.

A FIGHTER, I GUESS.

OR MAYBE A BARBARIAN.

PROBABLY NOT A BARBARIAN.
OKAY, WISE GUY!

IF YOU NEED ME TO HELP JUNIPER ON THE FRONT LINES, I'M MORE THAN HAPPY TO CARRY THE SWORD.
NO. I DON'T THINK SO.
I DON'T WANT TO RISK LOSING YOU AGAIN.
BESIDES, IT'LL BE BETTER TO HAVE YOU FIGHTING FROM A DISTANCE.
WITH WHAT'S COMING, WE'LL NEED TO BE AS VERSATILE AS POSSIBLE.

SOLUSTERRA

UNDERGROUND FORTRESS TEN MILES BELOW KINGSHILL CASTLE
I'M SORRY I'M LATE, MY LORD. I OVERHEARD TRAVIS AND JUNIPER TALKING ABOUT TRAINING, SO I FOLLOWED THEM.
UNFORTUNATELY, THEY DISAPPEARED AFTER ENTERING A PUBLIC RESTROOM.
THEY MUST BE TELEPORTING TO ANOTHER LOCATION FOR THEIR TRAINING SESSIONS.
ON ANOTHER NOTE, BELA HAS CLOAKED THE PORTAL LOCATED ON THE FARM IN HOPETON.
I ASSUME SO NO ONE ELSE CAN FIND IT. BUT THAT WORKS IN OUR FAVOR, TOO.

THE DOOMSDAY FORGE IS ALMOST COMPLETE. THE ONLY PIECE I NEED IS THE LEGENDARY SWORD OF LEGENDS.

I KNOW, MY LORD. I'VE LET YOU DOWN IN THE PAST, BUT IT WILL NEVER HAPPEN AGAIN.

WITH THAT SAID, I MUST HUMBLY ASK FOR YOUR ASSISTANCE.

TRAVIS DAVENTHORPE HAS TOO MUCH PROTECTION. I NEED HELP.

DO YOU HAVE ANY OTHER WEAPONS I CAN USE?

HA HA HA HA HA HA HA HA HA HA

YOU INSULT ME, ROGUE! OF COURSE I HAVE A WEAPON YOU CAN USE.

MANY WEAPONS.

THANK YOU, MY LORD.
LAST TIME, I GAVE YOU A **SOLDIER** AND YOU FAILED.

SO, THIS TIME, I'M GIVING YOU AN **ARMY**.

I PROMISE, MY LORD. THE LEGENDARY SWORD OF LEGENDS IS AS GOOD AS YOURS!
THE ARMY IS ALMOST READY.
BUT THEIR NUMBERS WILL BE TOO GREAT TO PASS THROUGH THE PORTAL ALL AT ONCE.
YOU MUST FIND SOME PLACE IN HOPETON TO HOUSE THEM AS THEY BECOME READY SO WE CAN DEPLOY THEM ALL AT ONCE WHEN IT IS TIME.
EXCELLENT! PERHAPS THE LARGE SHOW OF FORCE WILL CAUSE DAVENTHORPE TO HAND OVER THE SWORD PEACEFULLY.
OR MAYBE YOU'LL JUST HAVE TO **KILL** THE BOY.
EITHER WAY, THERE'S NO WAY YOU CAN FAIL ME THIS TIME, ROGUE.

"BOBBY DROPS BACK TO PASS..."
FEED

"BOBBY IS JUST ONE STRIKE AWAY FROM HIS THIRD STRAIGHT NO-HITTER..."
FEED

"BOBBY'S PENALTY KICK COULD SEAL IT FOR AFC RICHMOND..."

FEED

FEED

FEED

BOBBY, WOULD YOU QUIT MESSIN' AROUND AND HELP ME SET THIS STUFF UP?!
VOOOSH!

WHAT'S ALL THIS FOR, CARL?

CAMERA SYSTEM, BOBBY. I WANT TWENTY-FOUR-SEVEN SURVEILLANCE ON THAT BLACK HOLE.
OIL

SOMEBODY DOESN'T WANT US TO KNOW WHAT'S GOING IN AND OUT OF THAT PORTAL.
WELL, THE JOKE'S ON THEM, 'CAUSE I'M A-GONNA FIND OUT.
OIL

AND WHAT ARE YOU GONNA DO WHEN YOU FIGURE IT OUT?
FEED

FEED
FEED
YOU KNOW, I HADN'T REALLY THOUGHT ABOUT IT.
HELP ME RUN THIS CABLE, WILL YA, BOBBY?
WHATEVER, CARL.
Z

TRAINING SESSION
POUGHKEEPSIE, NEW YORK

OOF!

WUD!

UGH!
SO STICKY!

ENOUGH!

I GOT YOU.
THANKS.

OH, MAN! MY NEURAL TRANSMITTERS ARE SHOT!
FZZT!
FZZT!

PERHAPS THAT'S FOR THE BEST. JUST FOCUS ON THE BASIC FORMS I'VE BEEN TEACHING YOU.

I DON'T KNOW...YOU'VE SEEN ME USE THE SWORD WITHOUT MY TRANSMITTERS. **I'M AWFUL!**

AND WITH THEM, YOU'RE NOT MUCH BETTER.

LOOK, LET'S JUST TRY ONE SERIES WITHOUT THE TRANSMITTERS AND SEE WHAT HAPPENS, OKAY?

FINE!

WONDERFUL! EVERYONE, TAKE YOUR POSITIONS.

READY! ATTACK!

THOOMP
THOOMP
THOOMP

KOOOOM

BLOCK!

ACHIEVEMENT UNLOCKED
PERFECT COUNTER
XP 25

SUPER KICK!
3 DAMAGE

WHAT?

TRAVIS, **YOU DID IT!** THAT WAS BEAUTIFULLY EXECUTED!

BUT THAT WAS JUST A FLUKE! THERE'S NO WAY I CAN KEEP THAT UP WITHOUT MY TRANSMITTERS.

ACTUALLY, DUDE, I DON'T THINK YOU NEED THEM.

THIS IS WHAT I'M TALKING ABOUT, TRAVIS. YOU'RE LEANING TOO MUCH ON YOUR TECHNOLOGY. YOU'RE **THINKING** TOO MUCH!

FAITH IS SIMPLY **TRUST.** YOU DON'T HAVE TO **THINK** ABOUT THE POWER THE CREATRIX HAS GIVEN YOU—SIMPLY **TRUST** THAT IT'S THERE! THAT'S WHAT YOU JUST DID!

THAT MAKES ABSOLUTELY NO SENSE.
IF I DIDN'T HAVE SO MUCH FAITH IN THE CREATRIX, I'D SAY YOU WERE HOPELESS.
RESET! LET'S TRY AGAIN!

THANKS FOR LETTING ME SHOP WITH YOU, BUTLERBOT. I DIDN'T WANT TO SIT IN THE CAR WITH DAD. HE LISTENS TO WEIRD MUSIC.
MY PLEASURE, TRAVIS! THOUGH I ACTUALLY ENJOY YOUR FATHER'S TASTE IN MUSIC. "JAM BANDS," I BELIEVE HE CALLS THEM.
YOU ONLY LIKE IT BECAUSE I PROGRAMMED YOU TO ADAPT TO THE PERSONALITIES OF THE PEOPLE YOU WORK FOR.
WELL, YOU HAVE TO ADMIT, EIGHT-MINUTE GUITAR AND MANDOLIN SOLOS ARE QUITE CATCHY!
THEY MAKE ME WANT TO STAB MY EYES OUT.
Young's MARKET

MAN, THIS PLACE IS PACKED!
EVERYONE IS STOCKING UP FOR THE IMPENDING BLIZZARD, I'M SURE.

MILK, BREAD, AND WATER. THAT'S ALL WE EVER GET WHEN A SNOWSTORM ROLLS IN.

BUT NOT ON MY WATCH!

WE'RE STOCKING UP ON CHERRY SODA AND SOUR-CREAM-AND-CHEDDAR POTATO CHIPS!
CHIPS

WHAT THE—
CHIPS

COFFEE
SNACKS
CERE
...AND WHEN CHAPMAN CROSSED UP MOCCIO?
BROKE HIS ANKLES!
—AND THEN WENT STRAIGHT TO THE HOOP! EFFORTLESS!
BEST GAME I'VE SEEN ALL YEAR!

WHA THA?
WHY OH? YOU AND YOU.
WHO IS?
HUH?

HEY, TRAVIS!

HEY THERE, DAVENTWER—

GAH!

HELLO, TRAVIS.

MY PARENTS ARE HERE SHOPPING FOR THE STORM, AND WE RAN INTO DEREK AND **HIS** PARENTS! SO WE'RE JUST WALKING AROUND TO PASS THE TIME!

COOL! SO YOU GUYS WERE TALKING ABOUT THE BIG SPORTS GAME, HUH? THAT WAS A GOOD ONE!

DID YOU SEE THAT ONE MOVE THE GUY DID WITH THE BALL?

AND THEN THAT OTHER GUY WAS LIKE, "I'M GONNA TAKE THAT BALL!"

BUT THEN THE FIRST GUY WAS LIKE...

"YOU BETTER NOT!"

OH, MAN! SO GOOD!

RIGHT. WELL. DEREK AND I ARE GONNA GO CHECK OUT THE MAGAZINE RACK.

ALL RIGHT! SEE YOU TOMORROW AT SCHOOL!

I DIDN'T KNOW SHE LIKED BASKETBALL.

TRAVIS, IS MS. JUNIPER YOUR GIRLFRIEND?

NO!

THAT'S GOOD. FOR A MOMENT I THOUGHT YOUR GIRLFRIEND WAS CHEATING ON YOU WITH THAT DASHING YOUNG MAN.

HOOORRRK!

IT'S JUST DRY HEAVES, EVERYONE! NO CAUSE FOR ALARM! I'VE SEEN TRAVIS DO THIS BEFORE!
HOOORRRK!

GREAT JOB DOCUMENTING THE GROWTH ON YOUR PLANT PROJECTS TODAY! JUST A REMINDER...
...YOU ONLY HAVE THREE WEEKS LEFT TO WORK ON YOUR CLIMATE REPORTS! **DO NOT** WAIT UNTIL THE LAST MINUTE!
SERIOUSLY! I WILL SHOW NO MERCY TO THOSE WHO WANT EXTRA TIME!
TRAVIS?

I DON'T UNDERSTAND WHAT I'M DOING WRONG.
WHAT SEEMS TO BE THE PROBLEM?

I PLANTED THE SEEDS AT THE CORRECT DEPTH. I WATER THEM EVERY DAY. I PLACED THE TRAY IN THE PART OF THE WINDOWSILL THAT RECEIVES OPTIMAL SUNLIGHT...
GROWTH TAKES TIME, TRAVIS. YOU HAVE TO BE PATIENT.

BUT MY PLANTS ARE THE ONLY ONES IN CLASS THAT AREN'T GROWING YET!

DON'T BE SO HARD ON YOURSELF. THIS ISN'T A RACE!

NOW PUT YOUR TRAY BACK IN THE WINDOW AND GET TO CLASS. YOU'RE GOING TO BE LATE, AND I HAVE A PLANNING PERIOD I NEED TO USE.
MAYBE IF WE HAD A STEREO WE COULD PLAY SOME CLASSICAL MUSIC TO ENCOURAGE GROWTH...
NO STEREOS.
SEE YA TOMORROW, MS. CROSBY.

TRAVIS, ARE YOU OKAY?
YEAH. JUST FRUSTRATED WITH MY PLANTS IS ALL.

OKAY. WELL. IF YOU EVER NEED TO TALK, I'M HERE.

THANKS, MS. CROSBY.

YOU'RE THE BEST.

I DON'T KNOW ABOUT THAT.

GRIFF
WHAT'S BELA'S DEAL? I MEAN, I FEEL LIKE I'VE GOTTEN TO BE A PRETTY GOOD SWORD FIGHTER!
WHAT DO I DO HERE? DO I FIGHT THIS BEAST?
YEAH. THAT'S A LARNUX.
PRETTY EASY TO BEAT, BUT THERE'S PROBABLY A BUNCH MORE OF 'EM OVER THAT HILL.

BELA KEEPS SAYING I GOTTA HAVE "FAITH"...

...BUT WHAT DOES THAT EVEN MEAN?

WHY'S HE GOTTA BE SO VAGUE?! JUST TELL ME WHAT I'M SUPPOSED TO DO, MAN!

ISN'T THAT THE THING WITH FAITH? IT'S, LIKE, HARD TO EXPLAIN AND STUFF?

WELL, THAT'S DUMB.
OKAY. WHAT JUST HAPPENED?
YOU BEAT ALL THE LARNUXES, WHICH UNLOCKED THE DOOR TO THAT CAVE!

IS THAT WHERE I'LL FIND THE SWORD OF JUSTICE?!
YUP!

CONGRATS, TRAVBOT! YOU'RE ON YOUR WAY TO BECOMING A **LEGEND OF GRIFF** PRO LIKE TRAVIS AND ME!

BELA KEEPS TELLING ME I GOTTA STOP LEANING ON MY TECHNOLOGICAL EXPERTISE.
BUT THAT'S KINDA MY THING!

AND THESE NEURAL STIMULATORS ARE A PERFECT COMPROMISE BETWEEN MY TECH AND MY NATURAL ABILITIES. THEY HELP ME FIGHT **EXACTLY** LIKE GRIFF!

WELL, NOT EXACTLY LIKE GRIFF.
YOU CAN'T SHOOT ENERGY BEAMS OUT OF YOUR SWORD WHEN YOU HAVE FULL HEARTS.
THAT'S BECAUSE I'M A HUMAN.
AND I DON'T MEASURE MY HEALTH IN HEARTS.
JUST SAYIN'.
THAT WOULD BE PRETTY COOL, THOUGH...
HECK YEAH, IT WOULD.

SO YOU GOT ANY OTHER ADVICE REGARDING THIS WHOLE "FAITH" THING?

NADA. I GOT NOTHIN'.

YOU'VE BEEN A WONDERFUL HELP.
IT'S WHAT I DO.

GRUMBLE

AT THE RISK OF MAKING THINGS WEIRD...

WHAT'S THE DEAL WITH YOU AND DEREK DEVERS?

WHAT DO YOU MEAN?

THE WAY YOU STOPPED HIM FROM CALLING ME DAVENTWERP AT THE SPEEDBALL GAME...

...AND THE WAY YOU TWO WERE WALKING AROUND TOGETHER AT THE GROCERY STORE. WHAT'S UP WITH THAT?

I DON'T KNOW. HE'S A NICE KID.

A "NICE KID"?
YEAH. HE'S MISUNDERSTOOD.

"MISUNDERSTOOD"?
I THINK SO. HE WEARS A LOT OF MASKS.

"HE WEARS A LOT OF MASKS"?
ARE YOU JUST GONNA KEEP REPEATING WHAT I SAY? BECAUSE IT'S SERIOUSLY ANNOYING.

HE IS MY MORTAL ENEMY, JUNIPER!

AND YOU ARE MY BEST FRIEND!

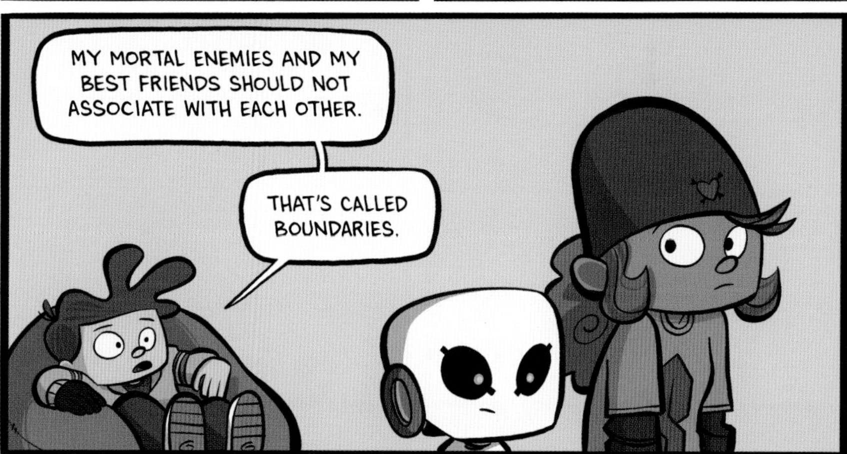
MY MORTAL ENEMIES AND MY BEST FRIENDS SHOULD NOT ASSOCIATE WITH EACH OTHER.
THAT'S CALLED BOUNDARIES.

OKAY, FIRST OF ALL, THAT IS NOT WHAT BOUNDARIES MEANS...

AND, SECOND, I UNDERSTAND WHY YOU'RE UPSET, TRAVIS. I REALLY DO.

OKAY, GREAT. SO YOU'LL END YOUR FRIENDSHIP WITH HIM IMMEDIATELY AND WE CAN ACT LIKE NONE OF THIS EVER HAPPENED.
NO. NOT QUITE.

I KNOW DEREK HAS BEEN AN AWFUL PERSON TO YOU, TRAVIS. AND I'VE TOLD HIM THAT.

BUT HAVE YOU EVER THOUGHT THAT MAYBE THE REASON HE'S SUCH A JERK TO YOU IS BECAUSE HE'S JEALOUS?

JEALOUS? OF ME? WHAT DOES HE HAVE TO BE JEALOUS OF?

A LOT, ACTUALLY.

YOU EXCEL IN SCHOOL, SO ALL THE TEACHERS ADORE YOU.
YOU HAVE FRIENDS WHO GENUINELY LIKE YOU AND AREN'T JUST SCARED OF YOU.

AND YOU HAVE A MOM AND DAD WHO LOVE YOU AND SUPPORT YOU FOR WHO YOU ARE, AND NOT WHO THEY WANT YOU TO BE.

WAIT...
WHAT?

IT'S EASY FOR SOMEONE TO BE YOUR "MORTAL ENEMY" WHEN YOU DON'T KNOW THEIR STORY.

OKAY, SO WHERE CAN I READ DEREK'S STORY? CAN I PICK IT UP IN THE SCHOOL LIBRARY?

YOU KNOW WHAT, TRAVIS?

OVER THE PAST COUPLE WEEKS, DEREK HAS SHOWN THAT HE IS **WAY** MORE OPEN TO DEALING WITH HIS FAULTS THAN YOU HAVE EVER BEEN THE ENTIRE TIME I'VE KNOWN YOU!

I CAN'T BE AROUND YOU RIGHT NOW.
I'M LEAVING.

IS THAT SUPPOSED TO MAKE ME FEEL BAD?
BECAUSE IT WORKED!
I'LL SEE YOU AT PRACTICE!
GRIFF

THE NEXT DAY...
KNOCK KNOCK

COME IN!

MS. CROSBY?

TRAVIS! HI!

I KNOW SCHOOL IS OVER, BUT I WAS HOPING I COULD CHECK ON MY PLANTS REALLY FAST.

SURE! I'M STILL WRAPPING UP A FEW THINGS.

THANKS, MS. CROSBY!
I'LL BE SUPER QUICK!
TAKE YOUR TIME.
IT'S NO PROBLEM.

OH MAN...

THIS IS
SO **DUMB**!

TRAVIS?
WHAT'S
WRONG?!

I CAN ENGINEER, BUILD, AND PROGRAM
ROBOTS, BUT I CAN'T GET A HANDFUL OF
STUPID PLANTS TO GROW!

THIS IS UNUSUAL BEHAVIOR FOR YOU. WHAT'S REALLY GOING ON?

I JUST TOLD YOU! I'M TOO **DUMB** TO GROW PLANTS!

OKAY. LET'S SLOW DOWN AND CATCH OUR BREATH.
AND ALSO, LET'S GO AHEAD AND REMOVE "DUMB" AND "STUPID" FROM OUR VOCABULARY.

TAKE A DEEP BREATH IN...

...NOW LET IT OUT.

GOOD.
FEEL BETTER?
A LITTLE.

I REALLY DON'T THINK THIS IS ABOUT YOUR PLANTS. WHAT'S ACTUALLY BOTHERING YOU?

I DON'T EVEN KNOW WHERE TO START. THERE'S SO MUCH GOING ON...

MAY I ASK YOU A BIG QUESTION?
SHOOT.

IS IT POSSIBLE FOR A SCIENTIST TO ALSO BE A PERSON OF FAITH?

WOW. "BIG QUESTION" IS AN UNDERSTATEMENT, BUT OKAY.

I'M SORRY.
IT'S STUPID.

NO! NO! IT'S NOT STUPID! STOP IT! PLEASE, SIT.

SOME OF THE GREATEST SCIENTISTS IN HISTORY WERE PEOPLE OF FAITH.

BUT THERE ARE MANY BRILLIANT SCIENTISTS WHO BELIEVE THAT SCIENCE AND FAITH DO NOT MIX.

SO, I GUESS MY ANSWER TO YOUR QUESTION WOULD BE "IT DEPENDS."

"IT DEPENDS"?

YES. IF YOU'RE ABLE TO SEPARATE YOUR FAITH FROM YOUR WORK AS A SCIENTIST, THAT'S GREAT.

BUT IF YOU'RE USING YOUR SCIENCE JUST TO PROVE OR DISPROVE A RELIGIOUS IDEA, THEN I'D SAY YOU'RE DOING IT WRONG.

BUT WHAT ABOUT **DOUBT?** HOW DO YOU DEAL WITH ALL THE JUNK YOU CAN'T **PROVE?**
WITH SCIENCE, WE HAVE ALL THIS HARD EVIDENCE...

...BUT FAITH HAS SO MUCH MYSTERY.

YEAH. IT CERTAINLY DOES.

FOR ME, THE MYSTERY OF FAITH IS THE MOST FRUSTRATING ASPECT OF BELIEF.

WHAT DO YOU MEAN?

I SHOULDN'T BE TALKING ABOUT THIS WITH YOU.
YOU DON'T HAVE TO GO INTO DETAIL OR ANYTHING...

sigh
I USED TO HAVE FAITH, TRAVIS. I USED TO BE VERY DEVOUT.

BUT... THINGS CHANGED.
I NO LONGER HAD PEACE WITH WHAT I COULDN'T EXPLAIN. SO FAITH STOPPED BEING TRUE FOR ME.

THAT'S FAIR.
YEAH.

WHERE ARE THESE QUESTIONS COMING FROM, TRAVIS?

LATELY, I'VE EXPERIENCED SOME THINGS. THINGS THAT I CAN'T REALLY EXPLAIN WITH SCIENCE.

HMM. MAYBE ONE DAY YOU COULD.

YEAH. I'VE THOUGHT THAT, TOO. BUT THEN I THINK THAT, EVEN IF I COULD, IT WOULDN'T CHANGE THAT THESE EXPERIENCES WERE SOMEHOW DIVINE.

I LOVE THE WAY YOUR BRAIN WORKS, TRAVIS DAVENTHORPE.

THANKS. SOMETIMES I FEEL PRETTY SILLY THINKING ABOUT THIS STUFF.

YOU'RE NOT SILLY.

YOU'RE JUST A KID GENIUS CARRYING THE WEIGHT OF THE WORLD ON YOUR SHOULDERS.

MORE LIKE THE WEIGHT OF THE **MULTIVERSE.**
WHAT?

NOTHING. I GOTTA GET TO CLASS.

THANKS FOR THE TALK, MS. CROSBY.
NO PROBLEM.
HE...ALMOST MAKES ME WANT TO FOLLOW THE CREATRIX AGAIN.
NO! I CAN'T GET ATTACHED.
I'M TOO FAR DOWN THIS PATH.

NICE! WELL DONE, JUNIPER! PERFECT DODGE!
WAY TO STAY LIGHT ON YOUR FEET!
IT'S REMARKABLE HOW FAST YOU CAN MOVE IN THAT ARMOR!
EXCELLENT MANEUVER, TRAVBOT! YOU'VE PREVENTED MY RETREAT!
WHERE'S TRAVIS?

HACK ATTACK!
WHAT ARE YOU DOING?
I'M ESTABLISHING A PERIMETER!
YOU OBVIOUSLY HAVE NO IDEA WHAT THAT ACTUALLY MEANS!

SHUT IT DOWN! PLEASE!
YUP!

WOOO! GREAT PRACTICE, EVERYONE!

JUNIPER, I THINK YOU'VE MASTERED YOUR MECH SUIT! YOU'RE UNSTOPPABLE!

TRAVBOT, YOU ARE DEADLY WITH THOSE SLIME BALL CANNONS. KEEP IT UP!

BELA...!
BELA, I GOTTA BE HONEST WITH YOU...

I'D LIKE TO SEE YOU GIVE MORE EFFORT.
ENOUGH!

FOR TOMORROW'S PRACTICE, I FORBID YOU FROM USING YOUR NEURAL STIMULATORS.

WHAT?! YOU CAN'T DO THAT!

AS A MATTER OF FACT, I CAN!

AND SHOULD YOU DECIDE TO DISOBEY ME BY USING THEM...

...I WILL BANISH YOU TO A PART OF THE MULTIVERSE THAT HAS NO VIDEO GAMES!

YOU CAN DO THAT?
THERE'S ONLY ONE WAY TO FIND OUT.

HOLD ON, BELA. ARE WE REALLY HAVING PRACTICE TOMORROW?
OF COURSE. WHY WOULDN'T WE?

WE'RE SUPPOSED TO GET A HUGE SNOWSTORM IN HOPETON TOMORROW.

SNOW ACCUMULATIONS ARE EXPECTED TO BE BETWEEN EIGHT AND TWELVE INCHES!

WE MUST TRAIN EVERY DAY. YOU KNOW THIS.

YES, BUT IT MIGHT LOOK REALLY SUSPICIOUS IF SCHOOL IS CANCELED BUT OUR FENCING PRACTICE ISN'T. WHAT WOULD WE TELL OUR PARENTS?

GOOD POINT.
I SUPPOSE WE SHOULD
PLAY IT BY EAR.

EITHER WAY, BE PREPARED FOR A
VERY LAST-MINUTE DECISION.

HERE'S A PORTAL BACK HOME.
EVERYONE GET A GOOD NIGHT'S REST.
C'MON, TRAVBOT.
LET'S GET OUTTA
HERE.

COULD YOU REALLY BANISH
TRAVIS TO ANOTHER PART OF
THE MULTIVERSE?

OH NO!
NOT AT ALL!

I CAN ONLY OPEN PORTALS WITHIN THE UNIVERSE I CURRENTLY INHABIT.

THE ONLY TIME I CAN TRAVEL BETWEEN UNIVERSES IS WITH THE CREATRIX'S HELP.

BUT TRAVIS DOESN'T KNOW THAT, SO LET'S KEEP IT BETWEEN YOU AND ME, OKAY?

¡ÓRALE! YOUR SECRET'S SAFE WITH ME, BIG GUY.

THE SOONER TRAVIS DITCHES THOSE NEURAL STIMULATORS, THE BETTER!
ATTAGIRL!

FEED
BALL!
TOSS!
FEED

FEED

FEED
THROW!

VOOSH!

BALL!
FEED

NO WAY!

BOBBY! PUT THAT FOOTBALL DOWN AND GET OVER HERE! YOU'RE NOT GONNA BELIEVE THIS!

WHAT IS IT, CARL?
FEED
OIL

WATCH THIS!
FEED
OIL

CLICK

FEED
OIL

FEED
OIL

FEED
OIL

THERE! DO YOU SEE THAT?!
FEED
OIL

NO.
FEED
OIL

LET ME JUST REWIND IT...
FREEZE FRAME...
ZOOM IN...
OIL

THERE!
OIL
FEED

DO YOU SEE THOSE WARPED SPOTS IN THE PICTURE?!
YEAH? KINDA?

LOOK AT ALL THESE TRACKS, BOBBY! WHILE WE WEREN'T HERE, SOMETHIN' CAME OUTTA THIS BLACK HOLE!

A LOT OF SOMETHIN'S.

DARE I SAY, AN **ARMY** OF SOMETHIN'S.

I FOLLOWED THE TRACKS AS FAR AS I COULD, BUT I LOST 'EM IN THE FIELD OVER THERE.

IF I DIDN'T KNOW BETTER, BOBBY, I'D SAY THERE'S SOME TYPE OF INTERDIMENSIONAL BATTLE THAT'S ABOUT TO TAKE PLACE RIGHT HERE IN HOPETON.

WERE YOU ABLE TO TRANSPORT THE ARMY I GAVE YOU TO THEIR HOLDING AREA?
YES, MY LORD. THERE WERE NO INCIDENTS.
EXCELLENT! WHEN WILL YOU ATTACK?

IN A FEW DAYS, AFTER THE STORM HAS PASSED...

NO! YOU MUST ATTACK IMMEDIATELY!

MY LORD, PLEASE. A DANGEROUS WINTER STORM IS GOING TO HIT HOPETON TOMORROW.

NOT ONLY COULD THE WEATHER BE DETRIMENTAL TO THE ARMY'S TECHNOLOGY, BUT VISIBILITY WILL BE COMPROMISED AS WELL!

FURTHERMORE, THE ADDITIONAL TIME MAY HELP ME DEVISE A NONVIOLENT SOLUTION TO OUR PROBLEM.
PFFT!
THERE'S NO TIME FOR PACIFISM.

THIS WINTER STORM MAY BE JUST WHAT WE NEED...

YES, I WANT YOU TO WAIT UNTIL THE STORM IS AT ITS **MOST VIOLENT...**

...AND THEN RELEASE THE ARMY! ATTACK WITHOUT PREJUDICE! CREATE TOTAL CHAOS!

ONCE THE BOY, HIS FRIENDS, AND THAT MEDDLING WIZARD HAVE BEEN DEALT WITH...
...BRING THE SWORD TO ME!

OH. AND ONE MORE THING, ROGUE.
YES, MY LORD?
IF YOU FAIL ME THIS TIME, **RUN.**
RUN AS FAR AWAY AS YOU CAN. TO SOME PLACE I COULD NEVER FIND YOU.
BECAUSE IF I DO FIND YOU, I WILL DESTROY YOU.
YES... MY LORD.

CHARGE STATION
MUTANT GUYS
ZZZZzz
tap tap tap
COMIX
COMIX

tap
tap
tap

tap
tap
tap

tap
tap
tap

BELA?!

I APOLOGIZE FOR DISTURBING YOU AT SUCH A LATE HOUR, TRAVIS...
BUT I WAS HOPING WE COULD TALK.
WOULD YOU CARE TO MEET WITH ME ON THE ROOF?
I CAN CAST A WARMING SPELL SO YOU WON'T BE COLD.
SURE!
Magic!
WHOA!

FOLLOW ME!
PRETTY COOL, HUH?

TOTALLY!

BUT... WHAT ARE YOU DOING HERE?

TRAVIS, I...
I NEED TO APOLOGIZE TO YOU.

FOR WHAT?

I'VE PUT A LOT OF PRESSURE ON YOU. TOO MUCH.

BUT NO ONE COMES TO FAITH BECAUSE SOMEONE YELLS AT THEM ABOUT IT.

I HAVE NO DOUBT YOU WILL FIND YOUR WAY, AND THAT WHAT YOU DISCOVER WILL BE WHOLLY UNIQUE TO YOU...
BUT MY INCESSANT BADGERING ISN'T DOING ANYTHING EXCEPT KEEPING YOU FROM FINDING IT ON YOUR OWN.
HOW CAN YOU BE SO SURE THAT I'LL FIND FAITH?
I CAN EXPLAIN, BUT IT WILL REQUIRE A BIT OF BACKSTORY...

MANY YEARS AGO, I LIVED IN AN ENCLAVE CALLED TEMPLEROCK WITH OTHER BRIGHT MAGES.
WE STUDIED THE TEACHINGS OF THE CREATRIX IN OUR HOLY BOOK, PRACTICED OUR MAGIC, AND LIVED PIOUS LIVES.

"WHILE STUDYING THE SCRIPTURES ONE DAY, I WAS FILLED WITH THE OVERWHELMING SENSE THAT THE PROPHECY REGARDING THE HERO OF SOLUSTERRA WAS ABOUT TO UNFOLD.
TOME OF LEGENDS

"AT THIS TIME, THE PEOPLE OF SOLUSTERRA WERE CRYING OUT FOR A KING. I FELT IT WAS NO COINCIDENCE THAT THESE CRIES FOR A LEADER WERE ARISING AT THE SAME TIME THE CREATRIX'S PROPHECIES WERE COMING TRUE."

AT THE BEHEST OF THE CREATRIX, I TRAVELED TO ANOTHER UNIVERSE TO FIND A NOBLE KING.
A KING I THOUGHT COULD BECOME THE LEGENDARY HERO FORETOLD IN THE PROPHECY.
WHY NOT LOOK FOR A KING IN SOLUSTERRA?
THAT IS A FAIR AND OBVIOUS QUESTION, TRAVIS. BUT THAT STORY WILL HAVE TO WAIT UNTIL ANOTHER DAY.
AS YOU ALREADY KNOW, THE CHOICE I MADE WAS MOST UNFORTUNATE.

WHEN NOL INVICTUS SHOWED HIS TRUE, EVIL COLORS, MY BROTHERS AND SISTERS AT TEMPLEROCK CHOSE TO REMAIN NEUTRAL. THEY GAVE ME A CHOICE:
RENOUNCE MY BELIEFS IN THE PROPHECY OR BE EXCOMMUNICATED FROM THE ENCLAVE FOREVER.
I CHOSE EXCOMMUNICATION.
WHY ARE YOU TELLING ME ALL OF THIS?

BECAUSE I WANT YOU TO UNDERSTAND THAT MY TRUST IN THE CREATRIX IS UNSHAKEABLE. THERE ARE TIMES I DOUBT, YES, BUT MY FAITH FAR EXCEEDS MY DOUBT.
I GAVE UP EVERYTHING TO FOLLOW THE CREATRIX.
I LEFT MY HOME. I FOLLOWED A MAGICAL SWORD TO ANOTHER UNIVERSE.
I BELIEVED THAT WHOEVER WOULD FIND THE SWORD WOULD NEED ME TO HELP GUIDE THEM TO THEIR DESTINY.
I ALLOWED MYSELF TO BE TURNED INTO STONE, TO LIE DORMANT AND IN SECRET UNTIL THE LEGENDARY HERO OF LEGEND ARRIVED.
AND NOW THAT YOU HAVE ARRIVED, I BELIEVE YOU WILL FIND YOUR FAITH AT PRECISELY THE RIGHT TIME.

I JUST WISH I HAD A SIGN. SOMETHING REALLY TANGIBLE, YOU KNOW?

THAT'S THE LAMENT OF ALL PEOPLE OF FAITH.
BUT, TRAVIS, YOU DO HAVE A SIGN THAT OTHER FAITHFUL LACK.
WHAT?

YOUR HAND, MY BOY! THAT MARK IS NO ACCIDENT. IT WAS PLACED ON YOU BY THE CREATRIX HIMSELF! YOU HAVE BEEN SET ASIDE, TRAVIS. CHOSEN BY THE MAKER TO DO INCREDIBLE THINGS! REMEMBER THAT EVERY TIME YOU LOOK AT YOUR HAND!
OKAY. I'LL TRY.

THERE IS A GREAT EVIL PERCOLATING IN HOPETON, TRAVIS.
IS IT NOL INVICTUS?
I'M CERTAIN OF IT. I FELT THE PRESENCE OF SOMETHING NEFARIOUS WHILE PATROLLING THE WEST SIDE OF TOWN NEAR THE GRAIN SILOS THIS AFTERNOON. I'M GOING TO INVESTIGATE THERE TOMORROW.
TRAVIS, I BELIEVE THE ROGUE IS STILL AT WORK HERE. AND THEY MAY BE CLOSER THAN YOU THINK.
BE CAREFUL.
I WILL.

WAKEY, WAKEY, EGGS AND BAKEY!
THANKS, BUTLERBOT! WOULD YOU TURN ON THE NEWS?
ABSOLUTELY!
CLICK

THE DAY WE'VE BEEN DREADING HAS FINALLY ARRIVED!
PHIL CONNORS – METEOROLOGIST
4

AS YOU CAN SEE, WE HAVE A HEAVY BAND OF WINTER WEATHER HEADED STRAIGHT FOR SOUTHERN OHIO.
WINTER STORM – LIVE UPDATES
4

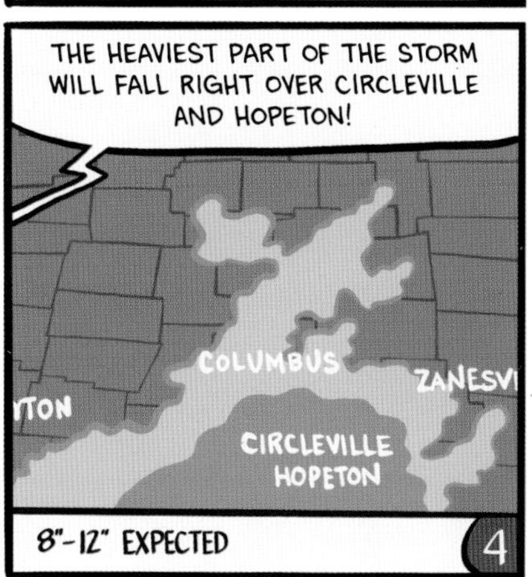
THE HEAVIEST PART OF THE STORM WILL FALL RIGHT OVER CIRCLEVILLE AND HOPETON!
COLUMBUS
ZANESVI
TON
CIRCLEVILLE
HOPETON
8"-12" EXPECTED
4

SNOW IS EXPECTED TO START IN THE EARLY AFTERNOON, WITH THE BULK OF THE STORM ARRIVING IN THE EARLY EVENING.
STORM WATCH
7P
6P
5P
4P
3P
PHIL CONNORS
4

MAKE SURE YOU HAVE A TRAVEL PLAN, AND—IF POSSIBLE—JUST STAY INDOORS!

WOW. LOOKS LIKE WE'RE REALLY IN FOR A MESS OF A STORM!

BAH! I'M NOT WORRIED.

YOU KNOW WHAT THEY SAY ABOUT OHIO WEATHER!

"IF YOU DON'T LIKE IT, JUST WAIT FIVE MINUTES."

YOU KNOW, BECAUSE THE WEATHER CHANGES SO FAST AROUND HERE.
WE GET IT, DEAR.

FORTUNATELY, TRAVIS AND I WENT SHOPPING TO STOCK UP ON NECESSITIES IN CASE WE GET SNOWED IN!
YOU'LL BE HAPPY TO KNOW WE HAVE ENOUGH CHERRY SODA AND SOUR-CREAM-AND-CHEDDAR CHIPS TO LAST US A COUPLE WEEKS!
THAT'S A LOT OF SUGAR AND CARBOHYDRATES!
EXACTLY WHAT THE BODY NEEDS IN A TIME OF CRISIS, MOM.

GRAIN SILOS
WEST HOPETON

WHA?

BLOCKED! I CAN'T SENSE ANYTHING!

THE SILO HAS BEEN CLOAKED MAGICALLY, AND I THINK I KNOW THE CULPRIT.

WHAT ARE YOU HIDING FROM ME, ROGUE?

ATTENTION, FACULTY AND STUDENTS.
IN LIGHT OF THE INCOMING WINTER STORM THAT IS ALREADY HITTING THE SOUTHWEST SIDE OF THE STATE, WE ARE RELEASING STUDENTS IMMEDIATELY. FURTHERMORE, THERE WILL BE NO SCHOOL TOMORROW.
TEACHERS, PLEASE WRAP UP YOUR LESSONS FOR THE DAY.
STUDENTS, ONCE YOU ARE DISMISSED, PLEASE GATHER YOUR THINGS AND EXIT THE BUILDING IN AN ORDERLY FASHION.
BUSES WILL BE WAITING IN THE BUS LOT. IF YOU HAVE TO ARRANGE ANOTHER FORM OF TRANSPORTATION, THE PHONE IN THE SCHOOL OFFICE IS AVAILABLE TO THOSE WHO NEED IT.
OTHERWISE, PLEASE WAIT IN THE GYMNASIUM WITH MS. LOCKWOOD UNTIL YOUR RIDE ARRIVES.
THANK YOU, AND **GO TIGERS!**

¡CHIDO! WELL, THIS JUST TURNED INTO THE GREATEST DAY EVER!
NO DOUBT.

OKAY, CLASS! USE THIS EXTRA TIME OFF TO STUDY UP ON YOUR RUSSIAN CZARS!
WE WILL HAVE THE TEST AS SOON AS WE'RE BACK IN SESSION!
Rurikids 862-1598
Godunovs 1598-1605
Michael Romanov
Peter the Great
Elizabeth of Russia
Peter III
Catherine the Great

I'M GONNA STOP BY MS. CROSBY'S CLASS REAL FAST. I'LL ONLY BE A MINUTE.

OKAY. I'LL WAIT BY YOUR LOCKER SO WE CAN WALK OUT TOGETHER.
SOUNDS GOOD!

SCIENCE LAB
JOURNALING CLUB
MTG ON SATURDAY!
WILLIAM WATTERSON M.S. IS MAD ABOUT SCIENCE

HEY, MS. CROSBY! I WAS HOPING TO CATCH YOU DURING BIOLOGY, BUT SINCE SCHOOL IS BEING LET OUT I THOUGHT I'D CHAT YOU UP NOW.

I'VE HAD MORE TIME TO THINK ABOUT OUR CONVERSATION ABOUT FAITH AND SCIENCE, AND—

CAN I HELP YOU, YOUNG MAN?

WHERE'S MS. CROSBY?
SHE HAD TO TAKE A PERSONAL DAY. I'M MX. BEECHER, THE SUBSTITUTE!

DID YOU HAVE SOMETHING YOU'D LIKE ME TO RELAY TO HER? I'M WORKING ON MY END-OF-DAY NOTES RIGHT NOW!

NO. THAT'S OKAY. I'LL JUST CATCH HER NEXT TIME.

OKAY! WELL, YOU BETTER RUN ALONG.
YOU DON'T WANNA GET CAUGHT IN THAT SNOWSTORM!
They/Them
NICE TO MEET YOU, MX. BEECHER!

WEIRD. MS. CROSBY NEVER TAKES A DAY OFF...
IS MAD ABOUT SCIENCE

TRAVIS! JUNIPER! OVER HERE!

MEET ME IN THE ALLEY!

COME ON!

BELA,
WHAT'S UP? YOU
SEEM REALLY
FLUSTERED.
TODAY! IT'S
HAPPENING TODAY!

WHAT'S
HAPPENING
TODAY?

THE NEXT
ATTACK!

I INVESTIGATED THE SILOS ON THE WEST SIDE OF TOWN AND FOUND THEY WERE CLOAKED WITH MAGICAL ENERGY.
THE SPELL IS COMPLEX. BREAKING IT WOULD HAVE DRAWN TOO MUCH ATTENTION.

DO YOU THINK THERE'S SOMETHING IN THE SILOS?

YES! WHAT EXACTLY IT IS, I CANNOT SAY.

I CAN ONLY ASSUME IT IS SOME TYPE OF WEAPON THAT NOL INVICTUS WILL USE AGAINST YOU TO RETRIEVE THE SWORD!

WHEN YOU FACTOR IN THAT A VIOLENT WINTER STORM IS APPROACHING THIS VERY INSTANT...

...IT'S EASY TO SEE THAT THIS IS AN OPPORTUNE TIME TO LAUNCH AN ATTACK!

SO WHAT YOU'RE SAYING IS...

...WE'RE ABOUT TO EXPERIENCE THE **PERFECT STORM.**

SO WHAT DO WE NEED TO DO, BELA?
SERIOUSLY?! NO REACTION TO THAT AWESOME LINE?!

TRAVIS, I NEED YOU TO GO HOME AND GET TRAVBOT.
JUNIPER, YOU NEED TO GET YOUR MECH SUIT.

MEET ME AT THE MAINTENANCE GARAGE ACROSS FROM THE SILOS IN THIRTY MINUTES!
YOU GOT IT!
ON IT!

SEE YOU SOON, BELA!

WHO WERE THOSE WEIRDOS TALKING TO? I DIDN'T SEE ANYBODY.

TRAVIS! WHY ARE YOU IN SUCH A HURRY?! SLOW DOWN!
CAN'T, MOM! I'VE GOTTA GET READY FOR FENCING PRACTICE!
NOW HOLD ON JUST A SECOND! WHAT DO YOU MEAN YOU HAVE FENCING PRACTICE?
THERE'S A WINTER STORM COMING!

WHAT IN THE WORLD IS GOING ON?
I DON'T KNOW. BUT SOMETHING DOESN'T SMELL RIGHT.
TRAVBOT! IT'S GO-TIME, BUDDY!
OH MY! IS AN ATTACK IMMINENT?!

IT SURE IS!

ARE YOUR SLIME TANKS FULL?

YES! READY TO GO!
OKAY, I'M PACKING A COUPLE EXTRA VIALS JUST IN CASE. WHAT ABOUT YOUR BATTERY?
IT CURRENTLY HAS A CHARGE OF EIGHTY-THREE PERCENT.

THAT'LL HAVE TO DO. WE DON'T HAVE TIME TO TOP YOU OFF.
ZIP!

LET'S GO!

SORRY WE GOTTA RUN! WE'RE PREPPING FOR A HUGE FENCING TOURNAMENT! YOU KNOW HOW IT IS!
STOP RIGHT THERE, TRAVIS!

DON'T MAKE ANOTHER MOVE! SIT DOWN AND TELL US WHAT'S GOING ON.

I'M SORRY, DAD. BUT I GOTTA GO.
MAYBE ONE DAY I CAN EXPLAIN, BUT FOR NOW I JUST NEED YOU TO TRUST ME.
TRAVIS, NO!
COME BACK!

I'M CALLING JUNIPER'S PARENTS.
WHAT ARE YOU UP TO, TRAVIS?
4

WOW. I'VE LIVED IN HOPETON ALL MY LIFE, BUT I'VE NEVER NOTICED HOW HUGE THE SILOS ARE!
YES. AND THE FOUR SILOS CLOSEST TO US ARE FILLED WITH SOMETHING NEFARIOUS.
I NOT ONLY FEAR FOR **OUR** SAFETY, BUT FOR THE ENTIRE TOWN, AS WELL.

HOPETON GRAIN

NOBODY MESSES WITH MY TOWN!
WHAT DO THESE SILOS NORMALLY CONTAIN?
CORN GRAIN, WHEAT GRAIN, AND SOYBEANS.
WE BUY FROM LOCAL FARMERS, AND SELL TO FLOUR MILLS AND FARMS ALL ACROSS THE COUNTRY AND CANADA.
WE EVEN HAVE SOME CUSTOMERS IN THE UNITED KINGDOM!
W
MY DAD OWNS THESE GRAIN ELEVATORS, SO I KNOW A THING OR TWO ABOUT IT.

WHO ARE YOU? HOW DID YOU FIND US?
WHOA! PUT HIM DOWN, BELA!
IS HE A FRIEND OF YOURS?
WELL, I WOULDN'T SAY **THAT...**

HE'S MY FRIEND, BELA.
YOU CAN PUT HIM DOWN.
WHAAAA!

DEREK! WHAT THE HECK ARE YOU DOING HERE?!

I HEARD YOU AND TRAVIS TALKING TO SOMEONE IN THE ALLEY AFTER SCHOOL.

I DIDN'T KNOW WHO IT WAS, BUT I'M GUESSING IT WAS **MAGIC MAGOO** OVER THERE.

MY NAME IS BELAZAR, BUT MY FRIENDS CALL ME BELA.

YOU MAY CALL ME BELAZAR.

AFTER YOU AND TRAVIS BOLTED FROM THE ALLEY, I FOLLOWED YOU TO SEE WHERE YOU WERE GOING.
CREEPY.

IT WASN'T LIKE THAT!

THE TWO OF YOU WERE ACTING SUPER STRANGE, AND I HAD TO GET TO THE BOTTOM OF IT!

WELL, THERE'S NOTHING WE CAN DO ABOUT IT NOW.

THINGS ARE ABOUT TO GET INCREDIBLY DANGEROUS, SO I SUGGEST YOU STAY OUT OF OUR WAY.

HEADS UP, EVERYONE! THE ROGUE IS WALKING AROUND THE SILOS!

ONCE THE ROGUE REMOVES THE SPELL PROTECTING WHATEVER'S INSIDE THE SILOS, WE'LL MAKE OUR MOVE. FOR NOW, LET'S PREPARE.

WHA... WHAT SHOULD I DO?
YOU HEARD BELA. TRY TO STAY OUT OF THE WAY.

YOU CAN DO THIS. YOU CAN DO THIS. YOU CAN DO THIS.

HAVE FAITH, TRAVIS.

I THOUGHT YOU WERE GONNA STOP PUSHING ME ON THAT.
OPE! THAT'S RIGHT! FORCE OF HABIT!

AS YOU WERE.

HOPETON GRAIN

TONK!

CRRRRCCK!

YES! YES! AWAKEN, MY PRECIOUS SOLDIERS!

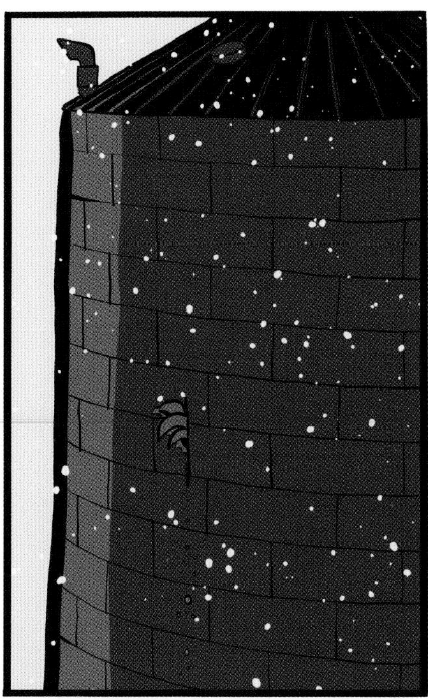

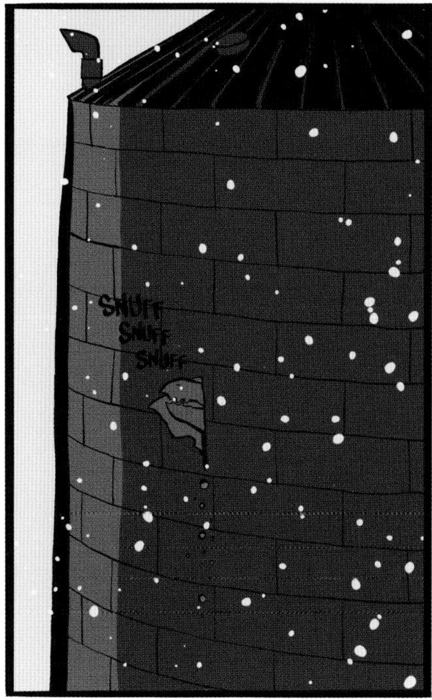
SNUFF
SNUFF
SNUFF

VELOCIBORGS

BOSS FIGHT

HEALTH: 2500 HP/ EACH
WEAKNESS: ???
SPECIAL ATTACK: TAIL WHIP

YOU ARE ALL SO BEAUTIFUL.
VELOCIBORGS! HEAR ME!
THE WEATHER IS FIERCE, BUT WE WILL USE IT TO OUR ADVANTAGE.
HOPETON GRAIN
THE MISSION OBJECTIVES HAVE BEEN UPLOADED TO YOUR MEMORY DRIVES.

FAILURE IS NOT AN OPTION.

YOU KNOW WHAT YOU MUST DO.
HISSSSSS

FIND TRAVIS DAVENTHORPE...

...AND BRING THE LEGENDARY SWORD OF LEGENDS TO ME.

LOOK AT THAT POOR FOOL, WALTER. OUT THERE IN THE WINTER STORM THROWIN' SNOWBALLS INTO THE BLACK HOLE.
HE'S OBSESSED!

NOW, I AIN'T NO PSYCHOTOLOGIST...
OIL

...BUT I'M PRETTY DANG SURE THAT BOBBY IS ASSERTING HIMSELF ATHLETICALLY TO COPE WITH THE EMOTIONAL TRAUMA OF HIS CHILDHOOD.
OIL

?
OIL

HE'S GOT DADDY ISSUES.
OIL

YOU KNOW WHAT? I GOT AN IDEA!
OIL

FOLLOW ME!
OIL

BOBBY! YOU GET INSIDE, YOU HEAR ME?! QUIT MESSIN' AROUND!
LET ME THROW A COUPLE MORE! I'LL BE IN SOON!

OIL

I'M PROUD OF YOU!
OIL

WHAT?!
FEED

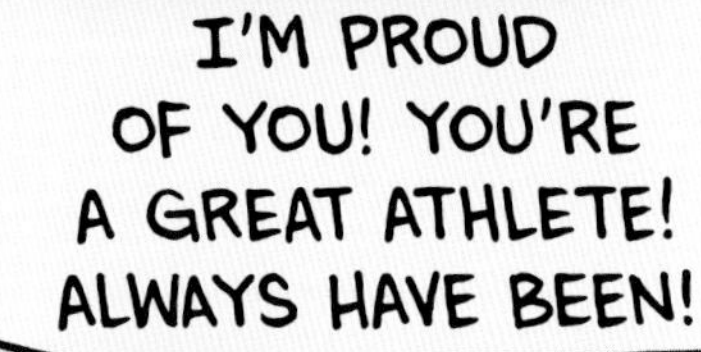
I'M PROUD OF YOU! YOU'RE A GREAT ATHLETE! ALWAYS HAVE BEEN!

ISN'T THAT WHAT YOU NEED TO HEAR? ISN'T THAT WHY YOU'VE BEEN THROWING ALL THESE BALLS INTO THE BLACK HOLE?

BECAUSE YOU NEVER HAD A POSITIVE MALE ROLE MODEL VALIDATE YOUR MASCULINITY?

NO.

I'VE BEEN THROWING ALL THESE BALLS INTO THE BLACK HOLE BECAUSE IT FEELS LIKE—IN MY OWN WAY—I'M LEAVING A TANGIBLE MARK ON A WORLD IN ANOTHER DIMENSION.
FEED

MAYBE SOMEONE ON THE OTHER SIDE IS NOTICING ALL THESE BALLS COMING OUT OF THE ETHER AND THEY'RE AMUSED BY THEM.

OR PERHAPS THE BALLS ARE FALLING WHERE THEY CAN'T BE SEEN, AND NO ONE WILL EVER KNOW I'M OUT HERE THROWIN' 'EM.
FEED

BUT **I** KNOW. AND THERE'S SOMETHING EXISTENTIALLY SATISFYING ABOUT THAT.
FEED

ALSO, IT'S FUN.
FEED

YOU CARE IF WE JOIN YA?
I'D BE DISAPPOINTED IF YA DIDN'T!

I REALLY AM PROUD OF YA, YA KNOW? I WASN'T JUST SAYIN' THAT.
THANKS, CARL.

WHAT ARE THEY DOING, TRAVIS? I CAN'T SEE ANYTHING! THIS SNOW IS **WILD!**
IT'S HARD TO TELL. THE ROGUE IS YELLING AT THE DINOSAURS, BUT I CAN'T HEAR WHAT THEY'RE SAYING.

GRAIN

THIS IS OUR CHANCE, TRAVIS. WE SHOULD ATTACK NOW WHILE THE ROGUE AND THEIR ARMY ARE VULNERABLE.

WELL, I'M NOT GONNA JUST COWER IN THE CORNER. I'M GOING WITH YOU GUYS!

NO! YOU'RE STAYING HERE!

THIS WILL BE TOO DANGEROUS FOR YOU. LET US HANDLE IT.

IF DAVENTWERP CAN FIGHT THESE GOOFS, THEN SO CAN I.

WHATEVER...

GET IT TOGETHER, EVERYBODY!
BELA IS RIGHT...

...IT'S GO-TIME!

ON THE COUNT OF THREE.
ONE...
TWO...

HOPETON GRAIN
GO! YOU HAVE YOUR ORDERS! FIND THE BOY AND FETCH ME THE SWORD!

UGH!
I KNEW THIS WOULD HAPPEN!

THIS IS **EXACTLY** WHY I WANTED TO WAIT UNTIL **AFTER** THE STORM TO ATTACK! THE WEATHER HAS COMPROMISED YOUR GPS TRACKERS!

CLEAR YOUR HEADS! WE MUST FIND THAT SWORD...

THREE!

WHAT THE—?

HOW DELIGHTFUL!
IT APPEARS OUR PREY
HAS COME TO US!

VELOCIBORGS!
ATTACK!

KRAK

BELA, YOU NEED TO CLOAK THE BATTLEFIELD! WE CAN'T LET THE NEIGHBORS SEE!
I WON'T LEAVE YOU ALONE WITH THE ROGUE!

YOU HAVE TO! I CAN TAKE CARE OF MYSELF! **HAVE FAITH,** REMEMBER?

FINE! BUT NEVER THROW MY TEACHINGS BACK IN MY FACE AGAIN!

KEEP THE VELOCIBORGS AWAY FROM THE PERIMETER! THIS SHOULD ONLY TAKE A MOMENT!
YOU GOT IT!

BRACE YOURSELVES AS I UNLEASH MY...

JUMP SLASH!

SPIN MOVE!

HACK ATTACK!

HAD ENOUGH ALREADY?!

IT SEEMS THEY'VE HAD ENOUGH OF YOUR **DREADFUL** FIGHTING STYLE.
HUH?!

HELLO, TRAVIS.
I NEED THAT SWORD.
GIVE IT TO ME.

YOU'LL HAVE TO PRY IT FROM MY COLD, DEAD HANDS!

IT DOESN'T HAVE TO END THAT WAY, TRAVIS.
NOW HAND ME THE SWORD.

NO! I WON'T LET NOL INVICTUS USE IT TO DESTROY THE MULTIVERSE!

YOU DON'T UNDERSTAND, TRAVIS! DESTROYING THE MULTIVERSE IS JUST THE BEGINNING!

NOL WILL RE-CREATE THE MULTIVERSE TO HIS LIKING! HE WILL MAKE ALL THINGS NEW!

I DON'T BELIEVE YOU!

HACK ATTACK!

Ting!
HUMPH!
-5

GIVE ME THE SWORD, TRAVIS. THIS CAN ALL BE OVER. YOU AND YOUR FRIENDS DON'T HAVE TO GET HURT.
PLEASE!
NEVER!

I DIDN'T WANT TO DO THIS, TRAVIS...

...BUT YOU LEAVE ME NO CHOICE.

AAUUGH!

KOOM

STAY DOWN!

YIELD.
YOUR FIGHT IS OVER.
IT'S OVER WHEN I SAY IT'S OVER.
BELA!
BZZT

YOU CAN FOLLOW THE CREATRIX AGAIN, ROGUE! IT'S NOT TOO LATE!
THE CREATRIX IS A **JOKE!** I FOUND MY TRUE POWER SERVING NOL INVICTUS!
NOL'S POWER COMES FROM TAK! YOU HAVE TO KNOW THAT!
THERE IS NO TAK, BELA. HE'S A MYTH THAT BELIEVERS IN THE CREATRIX USE TO SCARE PEOPLE INTO FOLLOWING THEM.

TAK IS **REAL.** BUT HIS POWER PALES IN COMPARISON TO THE MAKER'S. **TRUE FREEDOM** AND **TRUE STRENGTH** IS FOUND IN THE CREATRIX.
THERE IS NO FREEDOM IN FOLLOWING THE CREATRIX! FAITH IS A **PRISON!**

JUNIPER WAS RIGHT!
I SHOULDN'T BE
OUT HERE!

SNAARRRL

AUGH!

HISSSSSS

CHOMP
AAAUUGH!

HHUUURRRCK!

ENOUGH! YOU WILL NEVER GET THE SWORD!
NOT ON MY WATCH!
THIS ENDS NOW!

NO!

KA-KROOOOM

NO! BELA!

WAKE UP, BELA! PLEASE!

OH NO...
STOP!
STOP FIGHTING!

UHHHNN...
BELA, ARE YOU OKAY?! PUT THIS UNDER YOUR HEAD!
TRAVIS... YOU MUST...
YOU MUST HAVE FAITH.

I'M TRYING! I'M TRYING SO HARD!
THE CREATRIX TRUSTS YOU, AND...
...SO...
...DO I.
BELA! PLEASE! YOU CAN'T LEAVE ME HERE! I STILL DON'T KNOW WHAT I'M DOING!

BELA!

PLEASE, CREATRIX.
I CAN'T DO THIS ALONE.
I NEED BELA.

PLEASE.

BELA WAS WEAK. HE SHOULD NEVER HAVE OPPOSED NOL INVICTUS.

YOU KILLED HIM.

YES.
I DID.

AND IF YOU DON'T GIVE ME THE SWORD...

...I'LL BE FORCED TO KILL YOU, TOO.

I DON'T HAVE VERY MANY FRIENDS.
I CAN LITERALLY COUNT THEM ON ONE HAND.

AND NOW YOU'VE KILLED ONE OF THE BEST PALS I'VE EVER HAD!

I—I'M SORRY, TRAVIS.

PLEASE. HAND OVER THE SWORD. LET'S NOT MAKE THIS WORSE THAN IT ALREADY IS.

BELA TOLD ME THERE WOULD COME A TIME WHEN FAITH MADE TOTAL SENSE TO ME...

...BUT HE WAS WRONG.

OF COURSE HE WAS.

AND MS. CROSBY SAYS SCIENCE CAN'T PROVE FAITH...
...WHICH IS WHY SHE FINDS FAITH IRRELEVANT.

BUT THAT DOESN'T SIT RIGHT WITH ME, EITHER.

NO MATTER WHERE YOU STAND ON SPIRITUAL MATTERS, CERTAINTY ISN'T THE POINT.

FAITH IS ABOUT MYSTERY...
...AND CURIOSITY...
...AND **WONDER!**

I'VE RUN OUT OF PATIENCE, TRAVIS. GIVE ME THE SWORD, OR ELSE—
OR ELSE I'LL DESTROY YOU.

NO.

YOU'RE UNABLE TO DESTROY ME.

WHAAAAAAAT IS HAPPENING RIGHT NOW?
I THINK TRAVIS FINALLY BELIEVES...
SORTA.

ENOUGH!

THIS ENDS **NOW!**

YOU'VE BROUGHT THIS ON YOURSELF!
SHOOM!

ABSORB!

NEW ABILITIES UNLOCKED

NOOOOO!
RAAUGH!

SWORD CHARGE

HAAAHH!

OOF!
ZA-ZAPT!
SLIDE!
LET'S SEE IF YOU CAN DO **THIS.**

DID DAVENTWERP JUST FLY?

YEAH. AND HE SHOT ENERGY BEAMS FROM HIS SWORD.

HE MUST HAVE FULL HEARTS.

VSHOOM!

ACHIEVEMENT
EPIC GRAB!

Yank!
ACK!

CRUNCH!

WUMP!

SKKSSHHHHHH

WHAT?!

TRAVIS! PLEASE, LISTEN TO ME!

MS. CROSBY?! YOU KNEW ALL ALONG, DIDN'T YOU? YOU KNEW WHO I WAS!

TRAVIS, HE WILL NOT STOP! NOL INVICTUS WANTS THE SWORD, AND HE WILL DO WHATEVER IT TAKES TO GET IT.

I TRUSTED YOU! YOU'RE MY FAVORITE TEACHER!

I WAS WRONG, TRAVIS! SO MANY OF US WERE!

BUT BELA WAS RIGHT! YOU ARE THE PROPHESIED HERO! I SEE IT NOW, BUT BELA BELIEVED EVEN WHEN THE REST OF US COULDN'T.

I'LL NEVER FORGIVE YOU.

YOU SHOULDN'T.
WHAT I'VE DONE IS UNFORGIVABLE.

SO WHAT HAPPENS NOW? ARE YOU GOING TO KILL ME?

NO. I'M NOT LIKE NOL.

I'M NOT LIKE **YOU.**

NO. YOU'RE NOT.

I'M SO SORRY, TRAVIS!

VOOSH!

Sob!

LATER...
TRAVIS! YOU'RE OKAY!

THE ROGUE. ARE THEY... ARE THEY GONE?

YEAH. AND I DON'T THINK SHE'LL BE COMING BACK ANYTIME SOON.

TRAVIS, WHAT DO WE DO ABOUT THIS MESS? THIS WILL CERTAINLY DRAW UNWANTED ATTENTION.

YEAH. I KNOW. FIRST THINGS FIRST, THOUGH.

DEREK, MAY I SEE YOUR ARM?

UM, SURE. I GUESS SO.

TRAVIS USES HEAL 1!

DUDE! YOU HEALED MY ARM!

TRAVIS, WHAT HAPPENED TO YOU?

I REALIZED I WOULD NEVER HAVE AS MUCH FAITH AS BELA, AND THAT'S OKAY.

I THINK...**MY** FAITH DOESN'T HAVE TO LOOK LIKE **HIS.** MAYBE A LITTLE BIT GOES A LONG WAY.

SPEAKING OF BELA...

TRAVIS USES
REVIVE 1!

GASP!
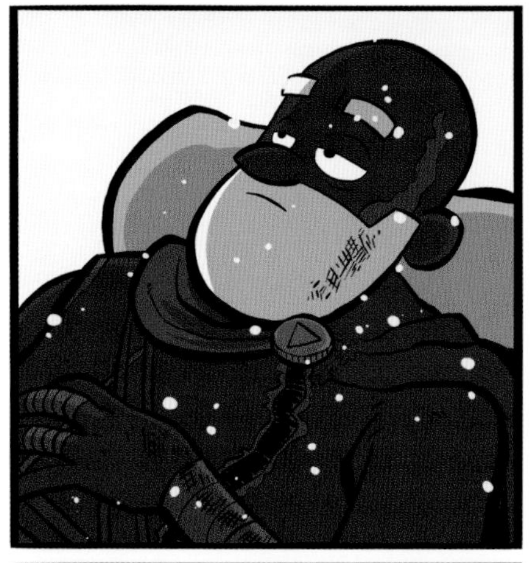

TRAVIS! YOU FOUND YOUR FAITH!

YEAH! SOMETHING LIKE THAT!

NOW WE NEED TO TAKE CARE OF THESE DINOS.

LET'S SEE IF THIS WORKS...

TRAVIS USES HEAL 1!

bing

HEY! CUT IT OUT!

I'VE FIGURED IT OUT! TRAVIS IS OUR PALADIN!
HUH?

IN OUR GROUP. YOU'RE THE TANK, BELA IS OUR SPELLCASTER, I'M THE RANGED FIGHTER...

...AND TRAVIS IS OUR PALADIN. HE'S A WARRIOR WITH A DIVINE CALLING.
TOTALLY!

AS SOON AS TRAVIS IS FINISHED, I'LL ESCORT THE VELOCIBORGS BACK TO THE PORTAL. I HAVE SOME EXPERIENCE LEADING CYBORG DINOSAURS DISCREETLY THROUGH DIMENSIONAL DOORWAYS.

IS THAT HOW THE CYBORG TYRANNOSAURUS DISAPPEARED THIS FALL?

OH. YOU'RE STILL HERE. **GREAT.**

YES, DEREK. THAT'S HOW THE CYBORGASAURUS REX DISAPPEARED.

I DON'T THINK THE MAGIC GUY LIKES ME.
HE DOESN'T.

YOU CAN'T TELL ANYONE ABOUT WHAT YOU SAW TONIGHT, DEREK!
NOT EVEN YOUR PARENTS!
RELAX, MY NERDS. THE SECRET'S SAFE!
MY HOUSE IS THIS WAY. I'LL SEE Y'ALL WHEN WE GET BACK TO SCHOOL.
LATER.
BYE, DEREK.

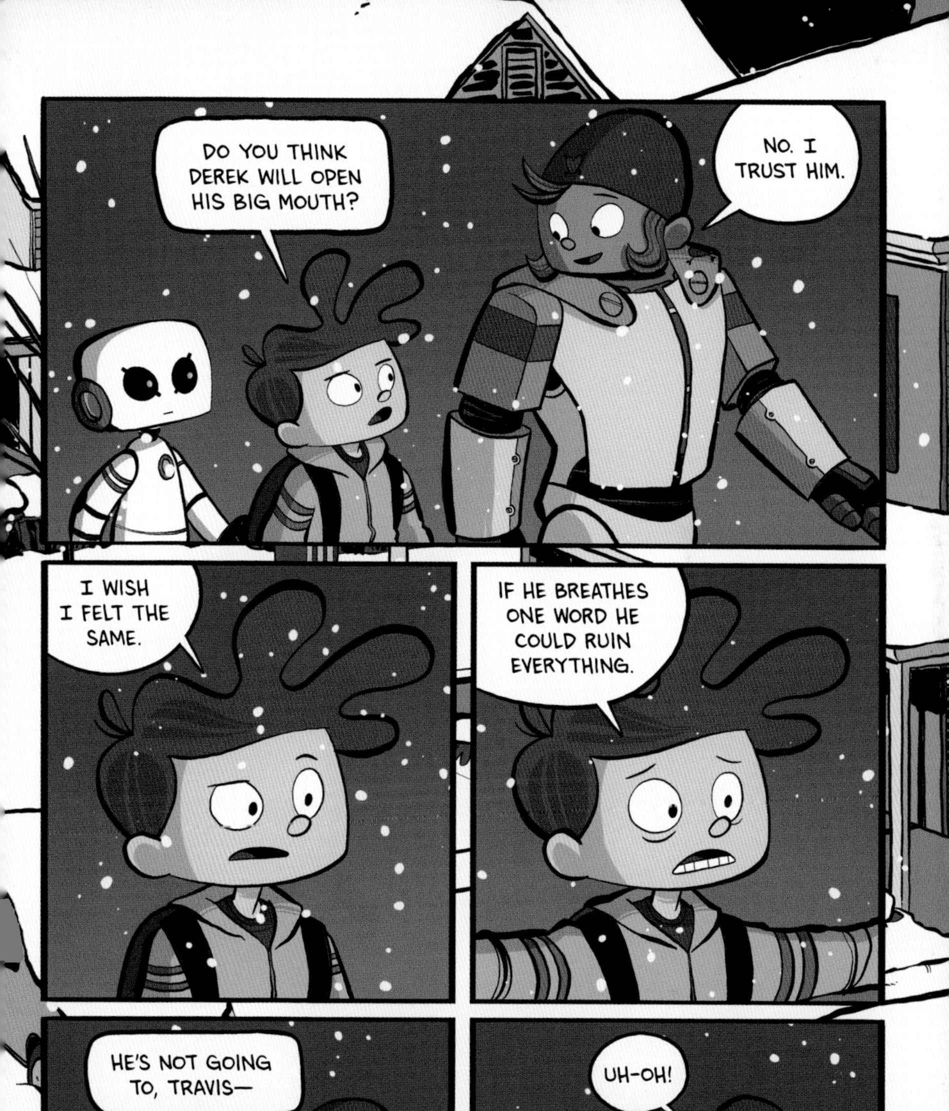
DO YOU THINK DEREK WILL OPEN HIS BIG MOUTH?
NO. I TRUST HIM.
I WISH I FELT THE SAME.
IF HE BREATHES ONE WORD HE COULD RUIN EVERYTHING.

HE'S NOT GOING TO, TRAVIS—

UH-OH!

THE JIG IS UP, GENTLEMEN.
REMEMBER OUR STORY: WE WERE AT FENCING PRACTICE, AND JUNIPER IS TESTING OUT A NEW PROTECTIVE SUIT SHE DESIGNED.

MOM. DAD.
MR. AND MRS. REYES.
WHAT ARE
YOU ALL DOING
OUT HERE?

YOU DISAPPEAR FOR HOURS IN THE MIDDLE OF A SNOWSTORM WITHOUT TELLING US WHERE YOU'RE GOING, AND YOU EXPECT US TO NOT COME SEARCHING FOR YOU?
YOU HAVE A LOT OF EXPLAINING TO DO, YOUNG MAN.

AND SO DO YOU, **JOVENCITA!**

TRAVBOT, I ALWAYS THOUGHT YOU'D HELP KEEP TRAVIS **OUT** OF TROUBLE!

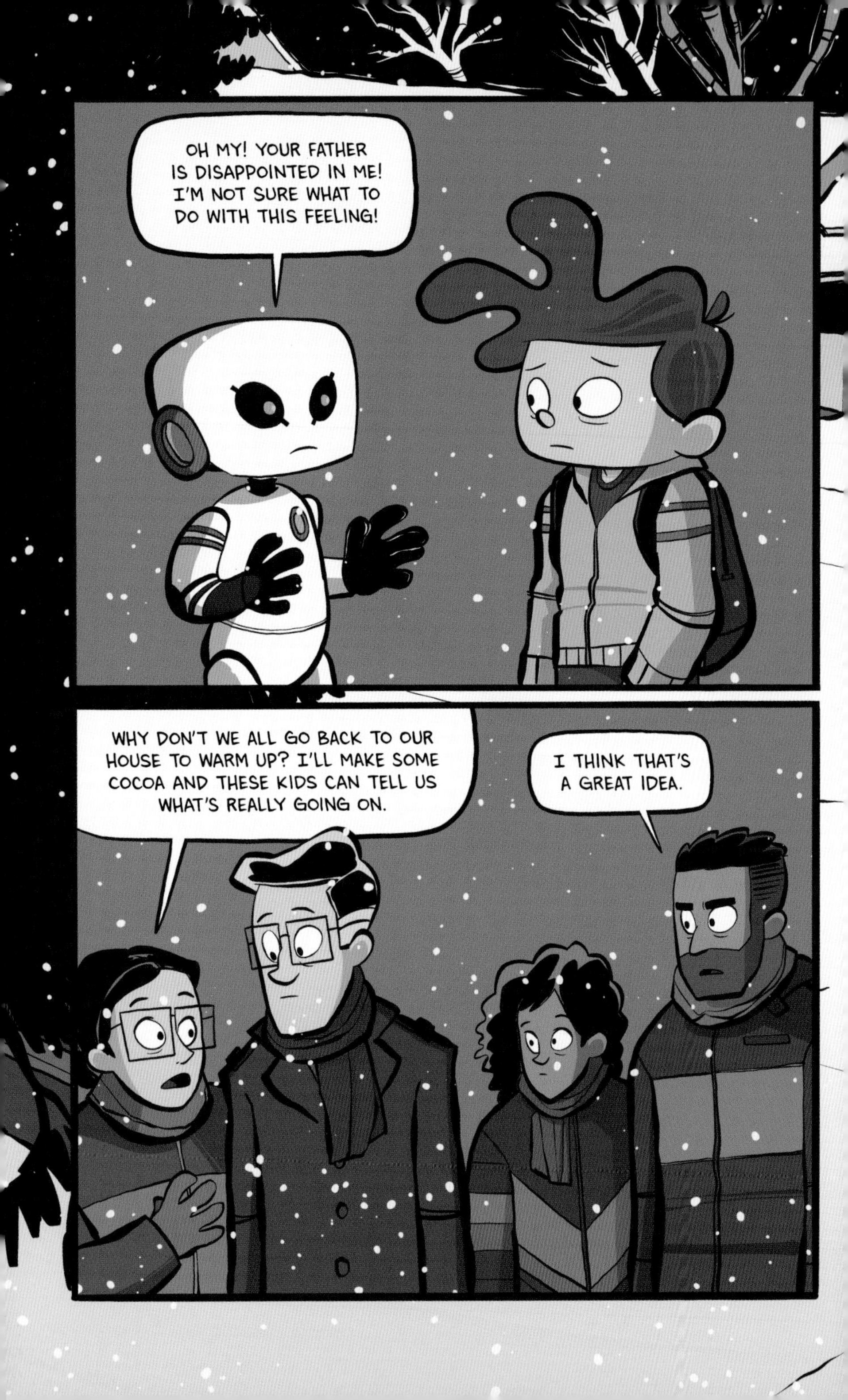
OH MY! YOUR FATHER IS DISAPPOINTED IN ME! I'M NOT SURE WHAT TO DO WITH THIS FEELING!
WHY DON'T WE ALL GO BACK TO OUR HOUSE TO WARM UP? I'LL MAKE SOME COCOA AND THESE KIDS CAN TELL US WHAT'S REALLY GOING ON.
I THINK THAT'S A GREAT IDEA.

AMERICAN LEGION
POST 291
HOW DO YOU COPE WITH YOUR FATHER'S DISAPPOINTMENT, TRAVIS? IT WEIGHS SO HEAVILY UPON MY CPU!
JUST EMBRACE IT, BUDDY.
IT'S GONNA BE A LOOOONG NIGHT.

THE NEXT DAY...
HOPETON VILLAGE PARK

HEY!

HELLO, DEREK! TRAVIS WANTED TO MEET WITH YOU, BUT UNFORTUNATELY HE IS QUITE GROUNDED.

SO IS JUNIPER. I TEXTED HER THIS MORNING AND SHE SAID SHE'D BE M.I.A. FOR A WHILE.

DID YOU GET INTO ANY TROUBLE WITH YOUR PARENTS, DEREK?

ARE YOU KIDDING? MY PARENTS DON'T KEEP UP ON MY WHEREABOUTS.
AS FAR AS THEY KNOW, I WAS IN MY ROOM DOING MY HOMEWORK.

OH. WELL. THAT'S GOOD, I SUPPOSE.

YEAH. I SUPPOSE.

I WAS TOLD TO GIVE YOU THIS. IT'S TRAVIS'S PERSONAL COPY.

Legend of Griff

ISN'T THIS THAT GAME ALL THE NERDS LOVE?

YES. AND TRAVIS SAYS THAT IN ORDER FOR YOU TO BE A PART OF OUR GROUP, YOU MUST LEARN WHY WE LOVE THIS GAME AS MUCH AS WE DO.

YEAH.
ALL RIGHT.

AND SINCE SCHOOL WAS CALLED OFF TODAY DUE TO THE SNOW, IT'S A PERFECT OPPORTUNITY TO ACQUAINT YOURSELF WITH THIS WONDERFUL ADVENTURE.

I'LL DO THAT, TRAVBOT.

OKAY, THEN! I'M SURE WE'LL SEE EACH OTHER AGAIN VERY SOON.

TRAVBOT!
HOLD ON!

YES, DEREK?
TELL DAVENTHORPE I SAID THANKS.
YOU KNOW. FOR THE ARM AND STUFF.
I WILL MAKE SURE TO TELL HIM, DEREK. HAVE A GREAT DAY!
SEE YA!

HOPETON VILLAGE PARK
DEREK DEVERS HAS JOINED THE PARTY!

SO HOW DOES IT FEEL TO BE A MAN OF FAITH AS WELL AS A MAN OF SCIENCE?
I DON'T KNOW. I DON'T REALLY WORRY ABOUT IT ANYMORE.
I'VE REALIZED THAT FAITH DOESN'T HAVE TO LOOK A CERTAIN WAY.
WHAT WORKS FOR ONE PERSON MAY NOT WORK FOR ANOTHER. AND THAT INCLUDES NOT HAVING ANY FAITH AT ALL!

FURTHERMORE, FAITH IS NEBULOUS! THERE ARE TIMES WHEN FAITH SEEMS ABSOLUTELY CERTAIN, AND OTHER TIMES IT SEEMS LIKE A COMPLETE FARCE.
BUT MOST OF THE TIME YOU DON'T REALLY KNOW.

MUCH LIKE THE TIDE, FAITH IS THE WATER THAT EBBS AND FLOWS IN OUR SOULS.

YOU'VE BEEN PRACTICING THAT SPEECH FOR A WHILE, HAVEN'T YOU?
YES.
I COULD TELL.

WHERE DO YOU THINK MS. CROSBY IS?

NO IDEA. SOMEWHERE THAT NOL INVICTUS CAN'T FIND HER. I CAN'T IMAGINE HE IS TOO HAPPY WITH HER RIGHT NOW. SHE'LL WANT TO BE AS FAR AWAY FROM HIM AS POSSIBLE.

SO WHAT NOW? ARE WE READY TO FIGHT NOL?

WE'RE CLOSE. IT'S TIME TO MOUNT FORCES FOR THE FINAL BATTLE.

ARE WE GOING TO SOLUSTERRA?!

NOT YET, BUT SOON!

IN THE MEANTIME, WE MUST CONTINUE OUR TRAINING. NOW THAT YOUR POWERS ARE FULLY REALIZED, TRAVBOT, JUNIPER, AND I MUST LEARN HOW TO COMPLEMENT YOUR ABILITIES IF WE HAVE ANY HOPE TO STAND AGAINST NOL'S MIGHT!

OUR PARENTS AREN'T BUYING THE FENCING RUSE ANYMORE. THEY KNOW SOMETHING'S UP.

PERHAPS IT'S TIME TO SHARE THE TRUTH AND LET THEM MEET ME.

YOU COULD COME OVER FOR DINNER! BUTLERBOT MAKES A DELICIOUS CHICKEN POT PIE.
NOT A BAD IDEA...

WHO KNOWS? MAYBE MY PARENTS AND THE REYESES WILL BE REALLY COOL ABOUT EVERYTHING.

...OR MAYBE JUNIPER AND I WILL BE GROUNDED FOR THE REST OF OUR LIVES.
WE'LL WANT TO AVOID THAT. BEING GROUNDED WOULD BE COUNTERPRODUCTIVE TO OUR PLANS FOR SAVING THE MULTIVERSE.

A
Hopeton Senior
THE END
(BOOK 2)

EPILOGUE I
HUFF
HUFF
HUFF
MY LORD! WE WERE UNABLE TO FIND ANY TRACE OF THE ROGUE.
BUT OUR GENERALS ARE CONFIDENT THAT SHE IS RUNNING FROM YOU AND WILL NOT POSE A PROBLEM TO YOUR ONGOING PLANS.

TELL ME, MINION...
WHERE IS THROK?

Y-YOU MEAN **THROK THE DEVASTATOR?**

WHAT OTHER THROK WOULD I BE TALKING ABOUT?

WELL, HE'S STILL IMPRISONED IN THE CAVERNS OF WYRN, MY LORD.

HE'S BEEN THERE FOR THE PAST FORTY YEARS, BANISHED THERE FOR HIS CRIMES BY TARVIS DRAGONTHORN BEFORE YOU WERE KING.

VERY GOOD. GATHER TWENTY OF MY STRONGEST SOLDIERS—
NO! MAKE IT **THIRTY!**
—AND SEND THEM TO RETRIEVE THROK.

HAVE THEM BRING HIM TO ME IMMEDIATELY.

MY LORD, MAY I SUGGEST ANOTHER WARRIOR FOR THIS TASK?

OR PERHAPS ONE OF OUR ASSASSINS?
NO!

THIS MISSION BELONGS TO THROK NOW.
AND I DON'T CARE HOW MESSILY HE COMPLETES IT.

EPILOGUE II

NOW, LISTEN, NIGE. I AIN'T NO ASTROPHYSICOO'...
ASTROPHYSICIST.
BUT I'M PRE'Y SURE 'AT RIGHT 'ERE IS A POR'AL TO ANUVAH DIMENSION.
WHA'EVAH, STAN.

PLAYER GUIDE

BELAZAR

(BEH-la-zar)

Bright Mage whose magical powers come directly from the Creatrix. Is helping Travis Daventhorpe develop his full potential.

VELOCIBORGS

(veh-LAWS-uh-bawrgs)

Velociraptors with mechanical appendages. Sent from Solusterra by Nol Invictus to help the Rogue steal the Legendary Sword of Legends from Travis, but Travis and his friends knocked them out of commission. Following his defeat of the Rogue, Travis revived all of the Velociborgs, making them docile.

DEREK DEVERS

(DER-ik DEE-verz)

Previously, the school bully and the bane of Travis Daventhorpe's existence. But now he seems to actually be . . . kinda cool? Maybe?

HOPETON (HŌP-tuhn)

A small village in rural southern Ohio founded by Thomas Hope.

JUNIPER REYES

(JOO-nuh-pur RAY-ehz)

An engineering genius who's best friends with Travis Daventhorpe. Following the destruction of her super-powered BMX bike, she poured all her energy and skill into an indestructible mech suit.

LEGENDARY SWORD OF LEGENDS, THE

(LEJ-uhn-der-ee sohrd uhv LEJ-uhnds, the)

An epic blade forged by the Creatrix himself. The sword is infused with mysterious powers and can only be carried by the Legendary Hero of Solusterra. Nol Invictus needs the sword to activate his doomsday machine that will destroy the multiverse.

MS. CROSBY

(miz CRAWZ-bee)

Science teacher at William Watterson Middle School. She is Travis's favorite teacher, and she is fond of him as an exceptional student. However, she is secretly the Rogue—a villain trying to thwart Travis's progress with the Legendary Sword of Legends.

ROGUE, THE

(rōhg, the)

Former Bright Mage who turned her back on the Creatrix to follow Nol Invictus. She now serves Nol Invictus as the king's spy and assassin by posing as Ms. Crosby at William Watterson Middle School.

MOM AND DAD

(mawm and dæd)

Travis's parents are pretty cool, as far as parents go. Their pride for their son is rivaled only by their naivete. Starting to get suspicious of his unusual extracurricular activities.

NOL INVICTUS

(nōl ehn-VICK-tuhs)

King of Solusterra. A harsh ruler who has turned against the Creatrix. Desires to destroy the multiverse and re-create it according to his purposes. No one knows where his power comes from, but there are rumors of a great evil that exists beyond the multiverse known as Tak . . .

SOLUSTERRA (SO-lus-tehr-uh)

A planet that is also a continent that is also a country in another dimension of the multiverse. Solusterra is loved by the Creatrix more than any other land in any other dimension he created.

CREATRIX, THE (cree-AY-triks, the)

The omniscient, omnipotent, and omnipresent deity who created—and continues to create—the entire multiverse.

TRAVBOT

(TRAV-bot)

The coolest little robot, boasting the most advanced artificial intelligence ever developed. Created by Travis Daventhorpe in his bedroom laboratory, Travbot is Travis's original best friend.

TRAVIS DAVENTHORPE

(TRA-vis DAV-en-thōrp)

Seventh grader at William Watterson Middle School. It's taken some time, but it appears he's finally accepted his role as the Legendary Hero of Solusterra. As a result, he's got some serious powers at his disposal!

WILLIAM WATTERSON MIDDLE SCHOOL

(WIL-yuhm WAH-ter-suhn MI-dul skool)

Small middle school located in Hopeton, Ohio. Named after the greatest artist and writer who ever lived in the history of the world.

THROK THE DEVASTATOR

(THRAWK the deh-vah-STAY-tuhr)

A wicked and brutal warrior who terrorized Solusterrans through robbery, kidnapping, and the like. Was finally brought to justice by Tarvis Dragonthorn and thrown into prison.

TARVIS DRAGONTHORN

(TAR-vis DRAH-guhn-thōrn)

Though never king, he was considered the unofficial leader of Solusterra during his later life. A skilled artificer, he was beloved by all Solusterrans. Following a cataclysmic event, it was he who saved the lives of countless dinosaurs by attaching robotic appendages and apparatuses to them. Was tragically killed in his workshop when a Brontoborgasaurus accidentally sat on him.

TAK (tack)

An entity of great evil that exists in the multiverse.

TRAVIS DAVENTHORPE
SIDE QUEST!
WELL, TRAVBOT. HERE'S THE DEAL...
AS PART OF OUR PUNISHMENT, DAD WANTS US TO FINISH THIS LIST OF CHORES **TODAY.**
WOW, TRAVIS!
ORGANIZE THE GARAGE?
CLEAN THE KITCHEN?
VACUUM AND DUST THE LIVING ROOM?
DO YOU THINK WE CAN GET ALL OF THIS DONE?
WE HAVE TO, TRAVBOT. IF WE WANT TO SURVIVE THIS GROUNDING, **WE HAVE TO.**
blip!
SIDE QUEST
FINISH THE CHORES
YESSSS! LET'S DO THIS!

UP

VRRRRMMMMM

THAT DOES IT, TRAVIS!
WE COMPLETED ALL
THE TASKS!

blip!
SIDE QUEST
COMPLETE
+50XP
SWEET!

OH, WOW. A NEW
EMOTE. I WONDER
HOW THAT WORKS?
UNLOCKED!
NEW EMOTE
RUNNING MAN

bing!
UNLOCKED!
NEW EMOTE
RUNNING MAN

WHOA!
LOOK AT ME, TRAVBOT!
I'VE GOT MOVES!

I'M NOT EVEN TRYING! IT'S JUST HAPPENING!

NOW I'VE GOT THE SIDE SHUFFLE!

BEING A LEGENDARY HERO SURE HAS SOME STRANGE SIDE EFFECTS.
I CAN DO IT BACKWARD!
END

GEOMETRY
TRAVPAD
cos(π/6)=√3/2
y=kx³ k>0
C=2πr
sin30°=½
sin45°=1/√2
sin60°=√3/2
k<0

THE ADVENTURE CONTINUES IN...

TRAVIS DAVENTHORPE GETS A LIFE!

Photo Credit: The Portrait Dude

WES MOLEBASH

(WES MoL-bash)

is the creator of several popular webcomics, most notably *You'll Have That* (Viper Comics) and *Molebashed* (self-published). He has also created cartoons for companies and organizations such as The Ohio State University, Target, and PBS Kids. *Travis Daventhorpe Powers Up!* is the second installment of his debut graphic novel series.